Praise for *The Disappeared*

"An elegiac, beautifully told memory-tale of obsessive love ... On one level, the novel is a young Canadian woman's bildungsroman; on another, a profoundly moving account of the genocidal horrors of the Cambodian killing fields and its terrible aftermath. Written in elegant, spare prose, *The Disappeared* confronts one of the most painful conflicts of our time: the collision between our private, personal desires and the brutal, dehumanizing facts of modern history."
—2009 Scotiabank Giller Prize Jury

"Echlin's masterful novel of meetings, partings and cross-cultural love ... Precise, expressive ... Powerfully vivid ... Luminous ... A complex expression of annihilating loss and eternal love that is best experienced, in a sense, like the final act of a tragic play: as something inevitable and beyond the calculations of reason."
—*The Globe and Mail*

"Echlin, one of Canada's finest prose stylists, approaches her subject with the delicacy and solemnity it deserves ... A beautiful work of art ... *The Disappeared* is an expert novel, which manages to penetrate to the aching core of the Cambodian tragedy."
—*National Post*

"Like her passionate narrator, Anne Greves, Echlin is not afraid to risk everything in this aching, heart-wrenching novel of young love aligned against human atrocity ... A slender book of remembering, *The Disappeared* is unforgettable."
—Sheri Holman, author of *The Mammoth Cheese*

"Powerful and moving."
—*The Times*

"Electrifying ... The voice is singular and arresting ... This is a very sensual book, written in an aroused but taut and plain prose ... Echlin's heroine is a risk-taker; so, on the literary level, is Echlin ... Through [her] technical and stylistic virtuosity, allied with elliptical narrative brilliance, Echlin raises Anne's climactic ritual action to a level of tragic sublimity."

—*The Guardian*

"The beautifully spare narrative is daringly imaginative in the details ... Echlin creates a sorrowfully compelling world ... [in this] powerful, transcendent love story."   —*Publishers Weekly*

"The familiar tale of star-crossed lovers is revisited with gripping immediacy and compelling freshness in Kim Echlin's *The Disappeared*. Writing with sensuality, yearning, and in a voice readers will not soon forget, Ms. Echlin reminds us of the potency of our first loves, and of their enduring ability to shape and haunt us."   —Stephanie Kallos, author of
Broken for You and *Sing Them Home*

"A beautiful elegy ... Anne Greves' story unfolds slowly, in spare and moving prose through fleeting moments and in floods of memory."   —*Winnipeg Free Press*

"A dance of words ... [full of] beauty, grace, sensuality and power ... In what is a seemingly impossible feat, the form is carved perfectly to the task—the book balances on the beauty ... Echlin is able, by imagination and art, to take the reader on a journey ... that travels into utter darkness but does not leave us in despair ... Echlin has wrought a work of singular beauty, a work which turns 'human cruelty' into the image of a particle of dust by a lover's cheek, into the rhythm of the sentences that carry knowledge of the world so all may witness."
—*The Chronicle Herald* (Halifax)

"Despite everything written about Pol Pot's regime in Cambodia, it is still possible to be deeply shocked by the stories

of two million who died in the killing fields, were tortured or simply disappeared ... Echlin has written a love story that exposes in terrible detail the consequences for generations of Cambodians living through 'Year Zero' ... An ambitious novel."
—*The Independent*

"Written with singular elegance, a polished, poetic, deeply affecting novel from a writer in impressive control of her craft."
—*The London Free Press*

"Daring ... Finely chiseled prose ... Undeniably beautiful ... [With] moments of genuine tension and power."
—*The Telegraph*

"A poignant love story and a memorable journey through a nation's troubled past ... Of all the tensions Echlin successfully negotiates in her novel—loss and recovery, betrayal and forgiveness, Eastern atrocity and Western indifference—the intersection of memory and language is the most nuanced ... Direct and devastating. She finds small acts of grace and dignity amid the suffering, and in this novel, it is these quiet gestures that speak the loudest."
—*The Walrus*

"[Echlin] renders the numerous Cambodians ... with a vividness and urgency ... The real story of *The Disappeared* is the author's longing to bear witness to buried lives ... Echlin succeeds, bringing to her work ... the 'infinite attentiveness that is love.'"
—*The Gazette* (Montreal)

"The impossibility of closure after great crimes, no matter how many tribunals and truth-and-reconciliation commissions we may launch, is the subject of Kim Echlin's absorbing new novel ... *The Disappeared* takes its place with such other chronicles of female desire as Elizabeth Smart's *By Grand Central*

Station I Sat Down and Wept or Pauline Réage's *The Story of O*, here yoked to a history that makes it both larger and more keen." —*Times Colonist* (Victoria)

"A beautiful work of art ... *The Disappeared* presents desire as an antidote to despair." —*Ottawa Citizen*

"Remarkable ... Radiant ... Echlin manages to juxtapose the horrific depravity of the Pol Pot era and its brutal successor against the power and resilience of individual human courage." —*The Calgary Sun*

"Echlin's pristine prose—there's a poet in there somewhere—evokes the pull of eros as Anne searches for the man she loves in one of the world's most dangerous places. But Echlin is equally skilled at portraying the effects of trauma on the human spirit ... *The Disappeared* does go to poetic lengths to come to grips with events too terrible to contemplate calmly." —*NOW*

"Terrific ... Well-crafted and moving ... With her spare—and unsparing—prose, Echlin does a stellar job of communicating the enormity of the Cambodian genocide through the prism of the personal." —*Edmonton Journal*

"[A] moving enigmatic story." —*More*

"[Echlin] summons the swirling passions of unfettered love, the blank panic of all-consuming grief and the devastating after-effects of holocaust ... with unsettling precision, making this novel a painfully emotional journey." —*Metro* (UK)

"Echlin has a vivid style all her own ... Spare ... Poetical ... It's a story which will live long in the memory, as much for the way Echlin writes as for the subject matter."
—*Newham Recorder* (UK)

PENGUIN CANADA

THE DISAPPEARED

KIM ECHLIN lives in Toronto. She is the author of *Elephant Winter, Dagmar's Daughter,* and *Inanna: From the Myths of Ancient Sumer.* Her third novel, *The Disappeared,* was nominated for the Scotiabank Giller Prize.

Also by Kim Echlin

Dagmar's Daughter

Elephant Winter

Inanna: From the Myths of Ancient Sumer

Elizabeth Smart: A Fugue Essay on Women and Creativity

The Disappeared

KIM ECHLIN

PENGUIN
CANADA

PENGUIN CANADA

Published by the Penguin Group

Penguin Group (Canada), 90 Eglinton Avenue East, Suite 700, Toronto, Ontario, Canada M4P 2Y3
(a division of Pearson Canada Inc.)

Penguin Group (USA) Inc., 375 Hudson Street, New York, New York 10014, U.S.A.
Penguin Books Ltd, 80 Strand, London WC2R 0RL, England
Penguin Ireland, 25 St Stephen's Green, Dublin 2, Ireland (a division of Penguin Books Ltd)
Penguin Group (Australia), 250 Camberwell Road, Camberwell, Victoria 3124, Australia
(a division of Pearson Australia Group Pty Ltd)
Penguin Books India Pvt Ltd, 11 Community Centre, Panchsheel Park, New Delhi - 110 017, India
Penguin Group (NZ), 67 Apollo Drive, Rosedale, North Shore 0745, Auckland, New Zealand
(a division of Pearson New Zealand Ltd)
Penguin Books (South Africa) (Pty) Ltd, 24 Sturdee Avenue, Rosebank, Johannesburg 2196, South Africa

Penguin Books Ltd, Registered Offices: 80 Strand, London WC2R 0RL, England

First published in Hamish Hamilton hardcover by Penguin Group (Canada),
a division of Pearson Canada Inc., 2009
Published in this edition, 2010

5 6 7 8 9 10 (WEB)

Copyright (c) Kim Echlin, 2009

Canada Council   Conseil des Arts
for the Arts   du Canada

*We acknowledge the support of the Canada Council for the Arts which last year invested $21.7 million
in writing and publishing throughout Canada.*

*Nous remercions de son soutien le Conseil des Arts du Canada, qui a investi 21,7 millions de dollars
l'an dernier dans les lettres et l'édition à travers le Canada.*

Manufactured in Canada.

ISBN: 978-0-14-317045-7

Library and Archives Canada Cataloguing in Publication available upon request from the publisher.

Visit the Penguin Group (Canada) website at **www.penguin.ca**

Special and corporate bulk purchase rates available; please see
www.penguin.ca/corporatesales or call 1-800-810-3104, ext. 2477 or 2474

Year Zero was the dawn of an age in which, in extremis,
there would be
no families, no sentiment, no expression of love or grief,
no medicines, no hospitals,
no schools, no books, no learning,
no holidays, no music:
only work and death.

NEW INTERNATIONALIST

For the woman in the market

Tell others.

VANN NATH

Montreal

1

Mau was a small man with a scar across his left cheek. I chose
him at the Russian market from a crowd of drivers with solic-
iting eyes. They drove bicycles and tuk tuks, rickshaws and
motos. A few had cars. They pushed in against me, trying to
gain my eye, to separate me from the crowd.

The light in Mau's eyes was a pinprick through black paper.
He assessed and calculated. I chose him because when he
stepped forward, the others fell back. I told him it might take
many nights. I told him I needed to go to all the nightclubs of
Phnom Penh. The light of his eyes twisted into mine. When I
told him what I was doing, the pinprick opened and closed over
a fleeting compassion. Then he named his price, which was
high, and said, I can help you, borng srei.

Bones work their way to the surface. Thirty years have passed
since that day in the market in Phnom Penh. I still hear your
voice. I first met you in old Montreal at L'air du temps, where I
went to hear Buddy Guy sing "I Can't Quit the Blues." I was
sixteen, and it was Halloween night. Charlotte and her friends
did not wear costumes, but I used the occasion to disguise my
age by putting on a shiny red eye mask decorated at the temples

with yellow and purple feathers. My long kinked hair was loose and I wore a ribbed black sweater, my widest jeans, leather boots. As soon as we were past the doorman, I pulled off my mask and I saw you looking at me. We took a round table close to the stage in the smoke-filled room. All through the first set I rolled cigarettes and passed them to the girls at my table and listened to Buddy Guy pleading the blues, eyebrows way up, eyes wide open, singing "Stone Crazy" and "No Lie," then squeezing his eyes shut he sang about homely-girl-love and begging-for-it-love, and I kept glancing over to see if you were looking at me.

I did not avoid your mud dark eyes. Between sets you stood, lifted your chair above your head and walked through the crowd toward me. You were slim and wiry and you wore a white T-shirt and faded jeans and your black hair was tied back at the nape of your neck. Your leather jacket was scuffed and your runners worn. You shifted sideways to let a tray go by and you said to the girls at my table, Can I join you? I brought my own seat.

The girls looked at each other and someone said yes and you put your chair in beside me, its back against the table. Charlotte said, You play in No Exit, I've seen you at the pub. What's your name?

Serey.

They poured you a beer from the pitcher and you talked in your soft voice to all of us. Asked, What are you studying? When you turned to me I had to say, I'm still in high school.

Charlotte said, I'm her Latin tutor. Her name is Anne Greves. You asked, Is Latin difficult? A girl across the table liked you and she said, I study Latin. You said you tutored math at the university. Said you'd seen them around, but not me.

Charlotte said, Her father teaches there and she doesn't want to be seen.

You smiled again and your front tooth had a half-moon chip and you said, Cool, in a strange accent of Quebec and English and something else I could not place.

The house lights went down. You leaned close and whispered, I want to touch your hair.

I did not say no or yes, but I felt the warm pressure of your palm against my skull. Then you put your elbows on the back of your chair.

You spoke with the mix of interest and inattention I was familiar with in men. Your excited eyes flickered to the stage, to the table you came from, to me. You wanted to know who was watching you. You wanted to see Buddy Guy and the horns and guitars up front. You wanted to watch me.

Years later you said, I remember watching you roll cigarettes with one hand. Fidgeting when the girls at your table talked. You seemed so free. I remember the light in your hair.

It was a time when young people from everywhere were driving Volkswagen buses through the mountains of Afghanistan and chanting in ashrams in India. But boys like you were not hippies or peaceniks or backpackers; colonized boys like you had always been sent abroad to study. You had been away for six years and you had learned to be at home in three languages, to navigate the manners and peculiarities of the West. Your education was mathematics and rock music. You knew functions and relations and your musician friends sang against war and had love-ins for peace. It was a time when young people believed the world could be borderless, like music. All this was naive, looking back. You were five years older, and you spoke a language I had never heard. And there was that animal feeling, the smell of your leather jacket, the quiver in my stomach, Buddy Guy's voice and your breath on my ear.

Years later you said, Do you remember in those days, the shock of an Asian guy with a white girl, or a black with white, or a French with English, all of us pretending nothing was forbidden? I never had the courage to ask a white girl until you, that night at L'air du temps.

Buddy Guy walked out for the last set in a green jacket that he took off while he played, hammering and pulling and bending strings with his left hand as he shook the right arm free, his right-hand fingers plucking and picking so he could shake off the left sleeve. His jacket fell to the floor and he grinned out at us when we clapped at his clowning. His mother had died that year and he said he was going to get a polka dot guitar in her honor but he did not have it yet. He played sounds he had heard other places and other times, horns and fiddles, concocting a New Orleans gumbo, a little of this, a little of that, paying homage to Muddy and B.B. and Junior. And then he got down to his own work. He sang about Lord-have-mercy-blues in "One Room Country Shack" and impatient love in "Just Playing My Axe," and with that great big charming smile he sang "Mary Had a Little Lamb," and about asking for a nickel from an angel and about strange feelings and broken hearts and, with a shake of his head, about women he could not please but we all knew he could please anyone, and I wished the lights would never come up. You put your muscled arm around my shoulder and pulled me close and you asked in a soft, soft voice, Can I take you home? A few people were dancing on the sides and you took my hand and pulled me up to dance too and you could sway at the hips but you had this way of moving your hands that was not rock and roll and not the blues but a small graceful bend backward in your wrist at the end of a beat.

Charlotte and the girls at my table were putting on their coats, pulling bags over their shoulders, flipping their long hair from inside warm collars like shirts flapping on a clothesline, and I said to them, See you.

We walked north on cobbled streets through the chill autumn air. You said, Would you like to come and see my band?

Maybe, I said. Where do you come from?

Cambodia.

Halloween revelers passed us, laughing and calling to each other in joual, hurrying through the darkness wrapped in black capes and devil masks and angel wings. Cambodia? I pulled my eye mask down.

You touched the feathers and said, Anne Greves, I like it here. Things are unimaginably free here.

I knew from that first walk home.

Outside my father's apartment on l'avenue du Parc I turned to face you and drew you under the iron staircase. You put your lips on my lips and I remember your eyes through the holes in my mask and the touch of your hand against my skull. You pulled me to you and I felt the first touch your fingers on my skin. Through the gratings on the stairs I sensed the movement of a neighbor boy with his Halloween basket, staring at us from the shadows, chewing on a candy-kiss. I caught his eye and said,

Jean Michel, pourquoi tu n'es pas au lit? Then I looked at you and said, *O malheureux mortels! O terre déplorable!* You laughed and released me, said, I want the whole world to see, and reached your hand up as if you were going to steal the boy's candy. Then we joined the child on the steps and you took a piece of string from your pocket and showed him a trick. There we were, an exile, a small boy and a girl-almost-woman, together in the darkness. I still hear your voice singing Buddy Guy's "I Found a True Love," and I remember how we sat that night and watched the clouds roll in across the moon.

2

Papa was a tall, husky man with thick hair and a shy smile that camouflaged his driven nature. He took me to a protestant church when I was a small child. I do not think he was a believer but I think he would have liked to be. He used to slide into the pew, close his eyes, drop his head and hold the bridge of his nose between the thumb and middle finger of his right hand. Watching him in this attitude of prayer I saw a man, unmasked and vulnerable, trying to be with his god. On the wall of the children's room in the basement was a picture torn from a magazine of a tall Christ with gentle eyes, standing in front of two sheep and a donkey, his arms around two children. This Christ's shoulders were a little stooped; he had a shy smile like Papa's.

I once complained to Papa about having no mother. He said, There are things we cannot change. One learns this: Get up, keep trying, you will find your way.

I listened and still longed for tenderness. I wanted him to say, I will help you. But he did not. He said, Think of yourself as a solitaire, a unique gem in the crown of the king, the philosopher's stone.

Why can't I be the gem in my own crown? I said.

He laughed then, his big Danish laugh. I amused him when I behaved most like him, determined, stubborn, and I was never afraid to be free, a thing I put down to my mother's early death. She had been a student in one of my father's classes. He was fifteen years her senior and I was the product of their late afternoon passion. There is something in the hard dying of the light on a frigid afternoon in Montreal that drives strangers to each other. My mother quit school to raise me, but when I was two, a truck crushed her car on an icy autoroute. Papa hired a French-Canadian housekeeper called Berthe Gagnon to take care of me. Berthe laughed easily, looked at me with fond eyes and filled my mother's absence. I am told that after a short time I did not miss my mother. But my father did. He was not interested in domestic life. Berthe went to my teacher meetings and took me to choir practice and watched my sports games.

Papa had no time for play. He had grown up poor and hardworking and ambitious, the only son of a Danish immigrant fisherman who died at sea on the Grand Banks when Papa was a boy.

My father liked to say, The war gave a poor boy like me a chance to be educated.

He was a tool and die maker and he had to beg to join the navy because they needed his skills at home. By the time he managed to get himself enlisted, the war was over. But he was lucky. He traded in his uniform with its handsome gold buttons and raised anchors for a veteran's education. He studied engineering and specialized in medical prosthetics.

It did not seem strange to me that he was rarely home. None of the fathers I knew spent much time at home in those years of rebuilding after the war. Papa liked his routines, mornings in the lab, afternoons teaching, evenings reading. He and my mother were together for only two years. I imagine them in that newly married state, each still trying to please the other. I imagine her charming him with her youth and her *joie*. After she died, Papa read to me at night when he got home in time and he took me fishing every summer for a week. He taught me the names of all the bones in the human body and I learned to recite them. He taught me to memorize Latin declensions, *amo, amas, amat*, and the Lord's Prayer in Latin, *pater noster, qui es in caelis*. He said Latin is the sign of a cultivated mind. I learned the prayers but not to pray. I learned to say I love you in a language my father called dead.

When he read to me he sometimes looked at the black and white picture of my mother on my bedside table. The focus is soft on the young woman holding a baby, me, and our eyes are locked together. Papa's voice would drift away and I learned to wait quietly until his attention flickered from the photograph back to the page. I think I began to read this way, studying the words in an open book, waiting for absence to be filled.

I have no clear memory of my mother. There is a photo of Papa and her standing behind a snowman on the mountain. His arms are wrapped around her waist and her eyes are laughing and her full lips are open in a wide, wild smile. It is cold but she does not wear a hat. Her hair is loose and long and windblown. I have her hair, kinked, gold streaked. I *do* remember lying on my back in the living room and the smell of warm cotton under her iron in the kitchen. And I do remember a black hole in the chill earth. I remember a lily in my hand, its white petals unnaturally waxen, someone called it Eve's tears. I was supposed to drop it on the coffin. I remember looking down and I was afraid of the depth and the hard lines of the cut earth.

This thing is sure: Time is no healer.

I remember fragments, bits of moving light on a winter wall.

Berthe took me to hear Etta James at a blues club on St. Laurent, on a night my father was away. She said, They can't see me bringing you in but once we're inside I know le gars, he'll let you stay. Alors, mon p'tit chou, you will come in with my groceries.

I pulled her grocery trolley with two wheels, its plaid sack attached to the frame. A block from the club, she helped me climb in, tucked a dish towel over my head and bumped me up two steps through the door.

Etta had a blond afro and a heart-shaped face and those huge painted black eyebrows and when she sang I was sure her eyes were looking deep into mine. She sang about blind girls and her lips were sad, and shrewd too. I knew that she cried like I did from a hidden place, ow, ow, ow, ow, as I listened to her talk-singing betrayals and epic quests for love, and I sank into the warmth of Berthe's lap, her arms around me, the woody scent of pine-tar soap on her skin. That night I under-stood why sound was first in the world, before even light or water.

Berthe was sent very young to work as a maid in an English-speaking house in Westmount. She looked at their art and listened to their music while she cleaned. She told me, That was worth more than the little money I got there, learning English and listening to Ray Charles and Robert Johnson.

At the end of my days at Miss Edgar's and Miss Cramp's school, Berthe and I used to lie on the floor together looking at the pictures on the covers of her long-playing records, listening to the scratch of Mississippi Delta blues and that ocean-deep Etta-voice pray-singing "Tell Mama" and "Sunday Kind of Love."

My father let Berthe go when I was thirteen because he said I did not need her anymore. She anticipated this and by the time she left she had taught me to cook for myself, to do my own laundry and homework. After school the thin winter sunlight disappeared into early darkness in our lonely apartment. I used to sit wrapped in a big eiderdown, reading under a single lamp with a chipped shade, the room's eclipse of the moon. I tried to get Papa's attention by letting my wild hair go wilder, wearing the tightest jeans, being the cleverest girl in my class. I bought some wire-rimmed granny glasses that neither helped nor hindered my vision. I told him I was going to friends' houses and sneaked into blues clubs until one night the owner of a little hole in the wall club in the north end stopped me when I was trying to slip in to hear Willie Dixon sing "I Ain't Superstitious." The doorman brought me to the manager's office and he called my father to come pick me up. Papa parked the car, walked past drug dealers and prostitutes and blues fans to the office, where I was studying musicians' signed photographs in cheap wooden frames on the manager's wall. On the drive home I told him it was unfair that I could not go inside, I had been taking the metro for years, listening to the blues for years. He nodded in a neutral way without taking his eyes from the road and said, It won't be long now.

I wanted him to say, I will take you. I will listen to music with you.

He hired Charlotte, one of his students, to tutor me in Latin, and as chance and my father had it, she liked the blues too and she started taking me along. I was an escaped green and yellow budgie protected by a flock of wild sparrows. Charlotte and her friends closed around me, standing in line for clubs, hiding this dangerously bright-feathered creature thrust upon them. And for a long time I felt that this was not an unsatisfactory way to grow up.

3

The snow the winter I met you was always blue. You came to fetch me on your old Harley at twilight, at the end of my dull days at Miss Edgar's and Miss Cramp's. The girls there spoke only English and were never allowed to come with me at night. They were mothered girls who invited me to spend weekends with them because I gave them cigarettes and told them about the clubs. I played recordings of Etta and B.B. for them in their chintz bedrooms with canopies and shelves of dolls and china. Their parents took us to the Ritz for Sunday brunches. But after I met you, I could not wait for the school days to end, to see you leaning against your bike in your worn leather jacket watching for me. I was always first out the door and I liked the girls' envying eyes on my back.

I swung onto your motorcycle and put my arms around your waist and we drove to the Yellow Door and listened to folk music and we drank coffee from thick mugs and I opened my books and did my homework and you marked sheets of math. One evening the back wheel of your bike skidded out on a bit of black ice. It crashed and I fell off and landed on my left shoulder. You jumped and landed upright and you lifted me quickly, then pulled up the bike and together we pushed it to the side of the road, where we shook ourselves off like a pair of pups. Our bodies were so light. Anything could send us hurtling through the air, steal us from each other, a patch of ice, a bit of bad luck. We got back on the bike that slippery night and kept riding, up the mountain to look at the city lights, down to the river to watch the ships.

What we shared was so simple. I remember thinking, I am so awake.

I came in late and my father said, The school called. They say he picks you up every day now. He is too old for you.

I shrugged, Not really. Boys my age m'ennuyent. You never mind when I go with Charlotte. She's older.

Your tutor, he said. That's different.

Oh, I said. Because you chose her?

My father studied me briefly. His beard had grayed. He turned away and said, Have you seen my glasses? He got up from his reading chair and walked toward the kitchen table.

I said, They're on your head.

He raised his right hand to put them back on his nose and I saw his beloved shy smile. He sat down again in his chair and looked at me over the half-glasses and said, You still live under this roof. You must listen to what I say.

When I was a child my father never argued with me. He would say absently, Go ask Berthe. But once, when I would not go to bed he said, All right then. Come sit with me. I will show you how many bones there are in a foot.

I remember his tenderness that night, his strong fingers tracing the lines of muscles and bones on my small foot, listening to the soft wonder in his voice. He said, No one has ever been able to duplicate the human gait. All we can really do is keep a person upright.

My father did not foresee what was going to become of me as a result of living with his drivenness. My father, my love, never stopped believing that he could lose everything at any moment, the curse of poverty. I was in danger of getting distracted from school, of not succeeding, of not marrying well. I think he believed that if he worked hard enough I could be shaped like a mechanical limb. He was afraid of my turbulence at sixteen.

I said, He is not too old for me. You do not even know me.

He said, No one talks to me like that. When did you become so cruel? Go to your room. Out of my sight.

I had no mother to turn to, and what I had learned from her was urgency. What I learned from my mother was that those we love can disappear suddenly, inexplicably. And then there is nothing.

4

You were so cool in your white shirt, speaking English and French with your band. You were on lead and there were three others, Luc on drums, and two brothers from Westmount, Ray on bass and Mark on a Hammond organ. You played covers of Santana and the Beatles, mixing it up with Junior Wells and Buddy Guy. I sat near the back and I watched the girls in the room watching you. When a boy asked me to dance I shook my head and Charlotte said, I will, and drifted away with him. You cradled and caressed the strings of that cheap guitar and I imagined your arms around me. At the end of the first set you came down from the stage and sat with me and I liked the eyes of the room on me too. You wore black jeans and your body was coiled-up energy and you were excited to be seen with me. Before you went back for the last set you leaned into my hair and said, I'm going to play something for you.

On stage you unwrapped a long-necked two-stringed Khmer guitar from a piece of brightly dyed fabric. You sat cross legged on a bench and lay the round body of the instrument on your lap. You looked into the crowd and joked, I am one of about seventeen Khmer in Montreal. People chuckled at your wry smile. You pulled the microphone down in front of the strings, said, But you're stuck with me. This is called a chapei, and we're going to play a song by Sin Sisamouth called "Don't Let My Girlfriend Tickle Me." You played a short, sweet melody, the hard calluses on each finger of your left hand pressing and releasing and sliding on strings over bone frets, your right hand loose, stretching out to pluck the notes. The band hit twenty funky electronic beats of guitar and chapei and organ and you sang campy rock and roll from the dance crazes and psych rock you had left behind in Phnom Penh. Your face smoothed around the Khmer words, and your voice slipped into a five-tone scale as you beat out a simple rock rhythm with your body and hammed it up.

You were a novelty, a charismatic Asian guy with a young white girlfriend and you sang from the open throated cool of the stranger. Young women were drawn to the gloom and glory of your exile, and Charlotte whispered to me, See that guy over there? He's a draft dodger. He's rattled by your new friend. Every eye in the room was on you. I wanted an exotic past too. You played your own version of "Black Magic Woman," half English, half Khmer, and then you put down your chapei and stood and lifted your hands and clapped to get the crowd moving and you said, This is "Lady Named No," and you sang in Khmer both a man's part and a woman's part in a thin falsetto, and no one knew what the words meant but we could all hear in your teasing voice a parody of asking and refusal. People were dancing and swaying and loving you. At the end of the set you said, This is a blues song I wrote in Khmer called "Sugarcane Baby." The words go something like: I can't get enough of your sweetness, baby, I'm just a boy peelin and suckin on white sugarcane.

People laughed and you knew you sounded charming speaking Khmer and French accented blues English and you looked down into the crowd at me and said, Je le joue pour Visna who is here tonight.

You picked up your chapei and you stopped camping it up and sang a sweet ballad in a voice that cracked and it was a song of love and it was the first time I heard the words oan samlanh. At the end Charlotte said, I have to fly. I think he likes you.

This was new, a man wrapping his feelings for me in a song.

People disappeared into the city night, left empty chairs twisted at odd angles from tables that smelled of beer. I waited for you in the doorway and breathed in the chill clean air. A few girls waited while the band packed their instruments, wound up wires, disconnected speakers. I put myself where I knew the light from a street lamp shone through my hair and when you came to me carrying your chapei and your guitar you were still excited from being on stage. You set down the guitar but holding the chapei you wrapped your arms around me from behind and said, Did you like your song?

I said, Who is Visna?

Visna means my destiny. The tune is a lullaby my mother used to sing to me, but I made up new words for you.

I never felt any forbiddenness of race or language or law. Everything was animal sensation and music. You were my crucifixion, my torture and rebirth. I loved your eyes, the tender querying of your voice in song.

After you left me under the stairs that night I ran up and through the front door and I did not want to break the spell of you but Papa called from his bed, You are spending too much time with him. Bring him to meet me Sunday afternoon.

I did not answer. People do not like to think of love as a crucifixion but I know now, thirty years later, that if a person is tough enough for love nothing less than rebirth will be required.

We walked past the front door to the musicians' entrance on rue St. François Xavier and the manager laughed when he saw us together and said, Hey, you found each other. He offered us a joint and we stood together looking out to the sidewalk. I can still see the manager's face, pock-marked and pale, and his nicotine-stained fingernails. He said to you, I listened to that chapei music you gave me. It's blues, man. Bring one of those guys here and I'll give him a show.

Inside, two old men sat in the hall, and we squeezed past them and found a table close to the stage. Thin university girls without bras blew smoke into the stale beer air and the place filled up. People were excited that night, waiting. The house lights dimmed and two spotlights made a thin halo over two wooden chairs. An old man walked from the back through a scatter of tables toward the stage. Another old man held the tail of his shirt and shuffled in behind. You said with reverence, There they are.

The two old men at the door.

One was near blind, the other lame. I watched them settle, adjust silver mikes, grumble at each other; one picked up a guitar, the other a harmonica, and with the thump thump thump of a hard shoe on the plank floor, air through metal and wood, fingers on tuned strings and a voice shout-singing, Whoo ee, whoo ee, the two stiff old men turned into the nimble,

golden-tongued blues gods they were, playing for their worship-
pers, embracing and breaking the hearts in that room, and I
could see how the world goes with no eyes.

My shoulder touched yours, transformed by what I heard
that night, syncopations, sound unbound and riffing, chat and
jokes and insults between left hand and right, between strings
and harp, slapping laughs and love moans and I heard things I
did not yet know but would, stories of humiliation and brawls
and seductions and nights gone bad and women weeping for
men and men lost and alone, music epic-great, born of sex and
police beatings and the stale beer stink of dark bars far away
from the churches of the towns.

We left the club in the first hour of morning and Sonny and
Brownie's affectionate squabbling on stage had sown in me an
idea about what happens when people last together a lifetime,
companionable grumpiness, separate cars, separate beds in
separate rooms, but out on stage chat-singing, their feet
pounding the same boards and their ears hearing the same
rhythms.

You said, I don't want to go home yet.

We rode your bike to the great river. Stars and water and
night. Down the riverbank, wrapped in darkness. You led me
along a dock where boats were moored in narrow slips and we
jumped onto the deck of a sloop called Rosalind. You took a
small key from your jeans pocket and unlocked the cabin door.
I followed you down three steep steps into a tiny galley and you
opened a cupboard door and took out a box of floating candles.
You said, At home it is Sampeas Preah Khe, the night we pray to
the moon. My grandmother always lit a hundred candles and
sent them out on the black river.

Why?

To honor the river and the Buddha.

You handed me a book of matches and I lit them with you, one by one. We sent out the ninety-ninth and hundredth out together and watched the trail of small flames drifting away. You said, My grandmother told me in the old days young people did this and prayed for love.

Inside the sailboat through the uncurtained window, I watched clouds moving across a sinking moon. Then I turned to you. You crossed your arms and pulled your white T-shirt over your head. I remember the muscled lines of your torso. Outside, wings and webbed feet on the surface of the water and the autumn wind rising and water lapping against the hull. Anyone walking along the river would have seen a hundred floating lights but they would not have seen any light at all from inside the Rosalind. I remember caught breath and a feeling no woman had ever admitted to me and the sound of a man's groan. I remember your eyes never leaving mine. I remember the roughness of the calluses on your left fingers on my skin and I remember how slow you were. It was early November on a night you called Bon Om Touk. I had not known there would be blood.

After, we slipped up to the deck naked. We jumped into the freezing water with small screams and came up laughing and trying to find our breath. Then we wrapped an old blanket around us and when I shivered you handed me my clothes and slipped back into yours and we rubbed our hair dry and you said, Look.

Our candles were still burning and drifting on the slow current, disappearing into the darkness where the river meets the sea.

23

My body pressed against your back, my arms around your chest, one of your hands on mine driving home that night, my cheek resting on your leather jacket. I did not go to my own bed in my father's house; I went to your apartment on Bleury Street with you. Through the hours before morning I loved you again in your warm yellow room, melting into you, standing up and lying down, heart to heart, our bodies golden heat and melting snow. Our fingers like small wings traced over each other's whispers all through that first night, the first night of life.

What is this scar on your temple? I asked, tracing its curve with my lips.

I fell on a rock at Sras Srang when I was teaching my brother how to catch frogs near the lake. That's how I chipped my tooth. I love how you talk. Tell me your name again.

The one who loves me called me Visna, I said. Do you like the name my lover gave me?

I love you with or without a name, Anne Greves.

I traced the shape of the half-moon chip on your tooth and whispered, I like Serey.

It means freedom, you said and pulled me to you again. It means power and beauty and charm. Do you like the name my parents chose for me?

I liked the hardness of your arms but I pushed you away, play-wrestling, and asked, All that? Does it mean good lover too?

You looked surprised, then said with your charming smile, Perfect lover.

You used to say that before me no woman ever teased you.

You were beloved and firstborn and I loved even your arrogance because now I knew you naked and vulnerable. I loved you on stage and I loved you walking beside me. But you were most truthful in bed. At dawn I dreamed of a lover whose body knows things she does not. I had lost my voice and we were in a restaurant called the Courthouse and I was calling for you but you could not hear. My father's presence was somewhere on the edges of the dream. You woke me and smoothed my hair and said, You are calling my name. Do not worry, oan samlanh, I will always be here.

The ocean has one taste and it is salt. I believed your body but I knew the words were untrue.

5

What do you have to say for yourself?

Nothing.

Nothing?

Papa set down his book and looked at me. Then he said softly, Your mother liked to wear my clothes when we first met.

A girl wears her lover's clothes because she likes his smell and she wears his clothes because she is trying to understand why she feels both freed and broken. Why does she feel whole when she has given away her body, her mind and her heart? Why is she not tempted to escape? She wants to smell her lover on her skin, and she cannot understand this feeling that imprisons, frees her. She does not guess that she will remember wearing her lover's clothes when she is old. She tells herself that what she feels is forever. But she has already observed in the world that it is not.

I turned away from Papa to go to my room, to be alone to smell your shirt, and then he said oddly, Do you still love me?

Of course I do, you're my father.

Then listen to me. He is not right for you.

Papa took off his reading glasses and wiped them on his sleeve and said, Your mother did not run around. Make a spectacle. Our neighbors talk. Your mother found invisible ways to get what she wanted.

I answered with intimate cruelty, Like the day she got pregnant with her professor and quit school. Like the day she left her baby and drove away in a snowstorm and never came back.

I knew one thing my mother would have wanted for me, her own desire—to live. The photograph beside my bed was changing; the twenty-two-year-old woman, her eyes locked into her baby's, seemed no longer tender but trapped. I wanted to give her the years she missed. I knew the one who took the picture; he left her long days alone, he sat reading long evenings through half-glasses and did not lift his eyes. I felt her ghost urging me, live, live for me, go, live, it ends at any instant, live, be free.

Maman, I did live. My only daughter was stillborn. (It has taken me thirty years to possess these eight syllables.) I tried. Even after Cambodia. Maman, I tried to live.

6

Papa sat at the kitchen table but did not get up when you came in. You stood waiting to be asked to sit down.

Papa said, What are you studying?

Mathematics. I tutor. I want to teach.

Do you like it here?

I have no choice. My country is closed.

You put your arm around my waist.

I slipped away from you, went to the counter, plugged in the kettle and brought three cups to the table.

Papa nodded to a chair, Go ahead. Sit.

You said to Papa, Anne told me you design prosthetics.

I teach in the faculty of engineering. We are working on a new leg right now, with spring, so a young amputee could learn to run on it.

You should have asked him to tell you more. Listened to him. Admired him. He would have talked and been happy and forgiven you your age and your race and your poverty. But you said, In my country we need legs that people can just walk on. In my country people fasten on wooden pegs.

Papa said, When will you go back?

You said with impatience, Our borders are closed. Nothing in. Nothing out. No one knows when things will open.

Papa looked gravely at you, Yes, I read about that. My father was an immigrant. He was a fisherman who came with nothing in his pocket.

Papa was ignoring me and you were sullen, and fleetingly I loathed both of you.

You said, I am not an immigrant. I am in exile. I do not choose to stay here. But I have no other place to go. My country is my skin.

Papa pushed back from the table and said, A person needs to be grateful to live somewhere.

He stood and said to me with raised eyebrows, I have some work to finish off.

And to you a brief nod, Pleasure.

Our cups sat empty and the water had not yet boiled.

Papa said, Do not throw it away like this. He will never be accepted here. Since your mother died, I have done everything for you. You must listen to me.

Papa had not heard you sing. He had not felt your touch. He did not know your tenderness.

I said, Papa, he already teaches at the university.

My father said, A tutor! He will leave you and go home. No good can come of a man who refuses to be grateful for shelter. He is too old for you. And anyway, no matter who he is, you are not yourself since you met that boy.

I would never be that self again. I was drowning in you. I would keep going back to you. Impossible not to.

7

After the first time, there is no rest. Every day we invented ways to be alone behind the closed door of Bleury Street. You picked me up at school and we went straight to your yellow room. You played tapes of Ros Sereysothea and Pan Ron and I listened to a chapei singer called Kong Nai. I heard Khmer rockabilly and surf and soul and two-stringed and four-stringed guitars and Farfisa electric organs and rock drumming and lyrics I did not understand. I did my homework at your kitchen table, humming Cambodian tunes under the photo of your family tacked on the wall and ate rice with you. I stayed overnight. I came and went as I pleased and I wore my father down. He swore at me and threatened to lock me in my room. But it was too late for that and when he had exhausted himself he said, You are stubborn. Even as a child I could not do a thing about it. You are a fool to ruin your life.

But a girl understands with her first lover that there is no daughter who does not betray the father, there are only great crashing waves of the woman to come, gathering and building and breaking and thrashing the shore. I watched my body's swelling and aching and flowing and shrinking as a sailor watches the changing surface of the waves. I let you do anything. I did anything I wanted and the dirty sheets of Bleury Street became my world.

The Saturday I am remembering, a snow faintly falling outside the window in a dusk half light, we were on your bed. We liked to smoke in silence, passing it back and forth, looking into each other's eyes, exploring our slight knowledge of ourselves. You delicately pinched the remnant heat into gray ashes between your thumb and long index finger and dropped it in a cup. Then you stretched your legs on top of the patterned yellow and purple Indian cotton bedspread and lifted your arm for me to lean against you. Together we watched the snow fall now brighter and slower against the deepening sky and I said, I think I can smell my mother, and you said softly, My mother used to make sticky rice wrapped in leaves for me and my brother to take frog hunting. We hunted them on the shore of the lake near the temple at Sras Srang. My grandfather showed me how to make offerings of leaves when the river changed direction.

I laughed, Changed direction?

The Tonle Sap flows south, then turns around and flows north when the snows melt in the Himalayas. That is when we celebrate the river festival, when it changes direction. We make boat races and have fireworks.

And send candles out on the river?

And kids throw firecrackers at people.

You smiled looking into that dark funnel of memory and said, My brother, Sokha, and I used to throw lit ones at lovers from the trees.

There was no one to ask how the borders of a country could close. You showed me the letters you wrote alone in your yellow room. You sent them to the Red Cross in the refugee camps along the Thai border and to the UN High Commission. We read *Year Zero* by a French priest called Ponchaud. He described people pushing hospital beds, women giving birth in ditches, a cripple with neither hands nor feet writhing along the ground like a severed worm to get out of Phnom Penh. You threw up in the toilet and then you opened the book at the beginning again and read all night, looking for clues about your family. In the morning you said, What if my family is dead? What if I can never go back? When we walked on St. Catherine you waved your hand in the air and said, Would Montrealers believe that soldiers could arrest anyone?

I told you about bombs that tore up the stock exchange and bombs in mailboxes and the mayor's house and men kidnapped and a politician left strangled in the trunk of a car for seven days. I told you how the police arrested Papa without charging him, only because he taught at the university. Criminal terror. Police terror. The front de libération du Québec. My father raged, Do they not see where force leads? He lectured to his classes, Force turns the one subjected to it into a thing. My teacher at school said, So what do we do, let the terrorists take over?

Even here, you said.

Why would here be different?

We watched a passing calèche, the horse's heavy breath a white cloud in the cold air. You asked, Why did they arrest your father?

They accused him of knowing how to build bombs. He told the police, I make legs and arms for people who lose them to bombs. He did not even speak French. Berthe stayed with me and I was terrified I would never see him again but they let him go after two days. I remember the paleness of his face the night he came home. He was not angry anymore. He held me and whispered, I was so afraid.

We bought a Sunday *New York Times* and the *Nouvel Observateur*. We took the papers to Schwartz's and outside the deli door a blind man with misshapen legs sat like a frog, feet splayed backward on a piece of cardboard. When he heard us walking nearby he said, I'm gonna take you to Hollywood, and you dropped a coin in his plastic dish. Inside we ate cheesecake and drank coffee. The papers reported mass slaughter in your country. You traced your finger over the newsprint and said, Sometimes they write millions dead and sometimes they write thousands. Don't they know? How can they sleep at night pretending to write facts when they don't know?

8

In the small black and white photograph of your family taped over the kitchen table you were sixteen and your brother, Sokha, was eight. You were taller than your father, who wore old-fashioned spectacles. I examined his hard jaw and saw the seed of your pride. One of your hands was behind your mother's back but everyone else's hands hung at their sides, formally. Your mother's clear face had the solitary look of a mother of sons. Your Vietnamese grandmother sat in the middle on a straight-backed chair, feet flat on the floor, everything at right angles like an Egyptian painting.

You said, Mak was fourteen when she was betrothed and married and she ran away from Pa's mother. But Pa was really in love so the second time she left he followed her and they ran away together from both families and promised each other they would work and find a way to buy their own house or they would drown themselves in the Tonle Sap.

Why does your little brother look so serious?

You laughed and said, He was angry at me that day. He asked me to let him play in my band but I told him he was too young, told him to clean our room and then I'd let him join. I was supposed to get my hair cut because they say there that long hair means a man is hiding something. So I got one of the guys in the band to cut it for me and I was running to the photographer's house late. I tripped and fell and cut my hand on the edge of a naga snake sculpture at the photographer's gate. It bled a lot and I covered it with a handkerchief and walked into the studio. My mother screamed when she saw the blood.

They wrapped it up in a bandage and the photographer told me to hide it behind my mother's back.

You rubbed your finger along a soiled edge of the picture. You said, Sokha will be almost fourteen now. Old enough to start his own band. Then you said, My mother tucked this into my pocket at the airport when I left and I laughed at her. It is the only picture I have.

Five people stare in a formal way into the camera. No one smiles. The tall boy has your eyes. The small boy has a shadow of a crease between his eyebrows and his eyes are stormy. The adults are composed. You looked from the photo to me and in your eyes' black pupils I saw already a survivor's pinprick of despair.

Then you stood abruptly and said, Let's go take our own picture.

We rode your bike to the train station and we went into the photo booth, pulled the black curtain behind us, smiled into the black glass and waited for the flash. We kissed and waited for the flash. We stood back to back with stern faces and waited for the flash. Then you put your hands into my hair and said, This one is mine. The machine sent out four photographs and you ripped the strip in half and you kept the last two and I kept the first two. You taped yours on the wall beside your bed and you got your guitar and sang "Hummingbird" to me. Then you said, I learned a new one, and you sang "Chelsea Hotel" in a talking voice. I laughed because certain music sounded so odd coming from you.

I said, I never ever thought of myself as little.

You said, annoyed, I never thought of myself not able to sing whatever I want.

I took your hands in mine and made you look at me and after a long time you said, Except for your hair you look a bit Asian. I like how you speak your mind and do not try to please me. Your mind is not Asian at all.

9

Bombs were dropping the length of the Thai border as you grew up. Tons and tons of bombs.

But in Phnom Penh, you said, we tried to go on as if there were no war. My father hired a chapei teacher, Acha Trei, for me. He took me once to hear the great chapei player Kong Nai, who was blinded from smallpox when he was a child. He was competing against the one-eyed chapei master, Phirom Chea. They sang rhymes and riddles to each other. Phirom Chea sang: *Two animals of the same name have three heads and nine legs.* Kong Nai sang back: *An elephant has four legs and a water elephant has four legs and a mango named Elephant Head lies in a dish.*

I said, But that is still only eight legs, and what is a water elephant?

The water elephant is a hippopotamus and the dish has a pedestal.

You sang it in Khmer, imitating two voices. I pretended to understand but I was on the untranslatable edge. You lay down your chapei and said, When I was thirteen I began to go around the city on my own and that's when I joined my first band. My best friend, Tien, was in the band. He played electric organ. We

listened to everything the American soldiers were bringing to
Viet Nam. I have not heard from Tien for a long time.

I took your chapei on my lap and plucked at the strings. I
imagined you in Phnom Penh listening to Western rock and
roll, absorbing the sounds and words brought by soldiers not
much older than you were. I said, Isn't it strange how people go
to war and still play each other's music?

You said, My grandmother used to take me to a temple to
pray for peace. I was afraid of the monkeys there. They snuck up
beside us and grabbed at the scraps my grandmother carried
wrapped in a cloth. She'd clap at them and then squeeze my
hand and say, If the enemy comes in front of you, make it pass
over. If it comes behind, make it disappear.

You reached across, took back your chapei, played a few
notes and hummed. You said, But after I started playing the
enemy's music I thought, I don't want to make the enemy disappear, I want to learn his music. And you joked, singing, The
enemy is in me, and I am in him.

10

We could survive a whole weekend on five dollars. There was always a bag of rice and we brought home fresh fish from Chinatown and fifty cents' worth of greens and a couple of oranges. We knew a café on Crescent Street where we could sit the whole afternoon with one coffee and we got into L'air du temps through the back entrance. Sometimes we walked up the mountain and threw snowballs over Beaver Lake and when our fingertips began to freeze we went into the churches. I liked St. Joseph's oratory best, its gloom and incense and hidden stairways.

You marveled at the high dark wall of abandoned canes and crutches, said, The Buddha believed only in the miracle of instruction.

We lit candles, not because we believed, but because we liked the flickering lights in tiers under crosses and icons, and we liked being together.

We wandered outside the oratory to the little house where the healer Brother André once slept on a hard, narrow bed. Through the glass panes we studied his brown robe hanging on a hook. You said, At home during Kathen festival, the people give new robes to the monks at the end of the rainy season. They stay three months in retreat, fasting and meditating. They make offerings to the ancestors until the people come and give them food and new robes. The monks live almost on air.

Like us, I said.

11

Montreal's dark winter afternoons lengthened into the translucent light of a northern spring and the snow melted and ran in long streams down the streets toward the river. From the top of the mountain the melt in the city looked like a great chandelier with strings of prisms. The first hepatica popped out of the ground and the first white-throated sparrow trilled *oo ee ee ee eeee*. You oiled up your bike and we drove through the chill air into the Gatineau, through Precambrian rock and thin pine into the endless idea of north.

We had so much time. I would soon finish at Miss Edgar's and Miss Cramp's and go to university and I said, Maybe I will live with you, and you said, Yes.

The last Sunday in March, after driving along the river to L'Assomption and back because a tank of gas for your Harley was cheaper than anything else we wanted to do, I sat at your kitchen table reading *The Golden Notebook*. From the stove, the warm nutty smell of rice cooking and you were gutting a fish. Rinsing the blood from your long fingers you said, Do you think my family is still alive?

I said without looking up, They must be.

Look at me.

I was startled by a sharp edge in your soft voice.

Do you think of what is happening there?

Of course I do.

I had been thinking about my book and communists and socialists in London who worked together and slept together and had children together.

I don't think you do.

Then you left the kitchen and walked down the long hall and came back with a yellowed telegram. You unfolded it and read: ARPIL 16TH, 1975, BORDERS MAY CLOSE. DO NOT COME BACK UNTIL I CALL. FATHER.

This is their last word, you said. Four years ago. Do you know what I did that day? I tried to telephone and the operator said there were no more lines to Cambodia. I went to the post office to send a wire. No lines. I gave the clerk a letter to mail and she said, I'm sorry. There is no more service. I dropped the letter in a mailbox outside anyway and four days later it came back to me with a stamp: undeliverable. Do you know what it means to send a letter to your family and read that it is undeliverable?

You stood holding the thin paper as if you could be swept away with a broom. I closed my book and put my arms around you and I traced my finger over your chipped tooth and we were two orphans standing in a forest and we left the pot of rice to burn and we tried to make love but we could not. There was never anything weak about you, your fingers were hard, your thighs were hard. Your skin was smooth as beach glass. I tried to soothe you, to rouse you, to make you forget but that day as you touched my hair you said, A person learns to imagine anything, oan samlanh.

Oan samlanh, my dearest darling. You taught me to call you borng samlanh, which is what a woman calls a man. Behind your charming smile, your fear was jammed and rusted. And after you finally fell asleep I crept out of your arms, wrapped up in a blanket, turned on a small light and read some more.

I saw the world more sharply with you, as if I had put on new lenses, the left a little stronger than the right, but worn together they shaped blurred edges into clear lines. There were moments I would have liked not to see so sharply. Borng samlanh, I wanted to know everything about you. I was young and but slenderly knew myself.

12

In April you said, I do not want to be apart from you ever.

And I knew you were going to leave.

Ares and wild boars and plowing. No one imagined what stench lay below.

I woke late and you were already up. The Sunday morning sidewalk smelled of spring, snowmelt and new green and car exhaust. I stretched my sated body on the sheets into the mild air and you sat on the edge of the bed and said, Oan samlanh, the Vietnamese invaded. The border is opening. I have to go back. I have to find my family.

I'm coming.

I cannot take you with me. You're too young.

(Why did you not strike me too?)

Too young? I have never been too young for anything you wanted to do. I am coming with you.

Anne, you cannot. There has been war there. I do not know what I will find.

I will find it with you.

You cannot come.

I got out of bed and threw on last night's clothes and I brushed you off me and ran down the steep stairs onto Bleury

Street and headed up the mountain. I sat by the lake and watched Sunday families, Sunday lovers, Sunday loners, filthy pigeons. I tried to imagine who I was without you. You had so much to do, didn't you? None of it you could do on a Sunday.

You came looking for me and when I saw you on the mountain I shed my raging body and already I was drinking your skin, combing your long black hair, wrapping myself around your narrow hips. Your eyes were determined but still pleading. I wanted the borders to close again, so I could have you back. I wanted you to die so I would not have to think of you without me. I wanted money. I wanted to be older. I wanted you to find your whole family alive so I could be with you. I wanted you to find your family dead so you would be mine. I wanted everything to change now, and everything to stay the same forever. I wanted to erase all transgression from my fate. You were salt and sweet, my whole body's desire. Under the unearthly clamor of the pigeons' insistent cooing all around us, the echo of my father's words, He will go home. All I wanted was to hear you say, I will wait for you. I will come back for you, but you said, The borders are open. I must go.

War claimed you.

13

Your ticket read: Paris. Phnom Penh. I wanted a ticket like that.

We made love before sunrise and left the house without speaking. I could not shed my anger at the airport.

Where will you stay?

At my parents' house, Phlauv 350. I will write.

When you reached for me, I pushed you away. You stepped back and you looked down at your watch, said, I am afraid of what I will find.

Then wait, and I will come with you.

Little tiger, don't be stubborn. Let's not leave each other without at least a kiss.

I am not the one leaving.

You were holding your chapei and I stepped into your arms and you buried your face in my hair. But then you walked through thick glass doors and turned once to wave and after a long time your plane slowly backed up and wheeled around and drove down the runway and disappeared into the air. I returned to the empty city and I went to my father's apartment and I felt blind and deaf and Papa in his reading chair said without looking up, Gone?

I waited for you. The first week I expected something every day, the second week turned into two months, six months, a year. No letter. No word. I sent letters to your parents' address. I tried to find a telephone number. I had my seventeenth birthday, then another and another and another and another. How could I have lost you? How could we have made love in the first gray light before dawn and then I would never see you again?

Papa said, Perhaps he thinks it is easier this way.

Charlotte said, Things were awful there. Maybe he needs time.

Berthe said, Don't worry, mon p'tit chou. You will find each other again.

She helped me find a part-time job selling flowers on St. Laurent in a shop called the Parisian. I had my own money. I went to the university and I studied languages. I was seduced by the shapes of words in my mouth and when I wrote them on the page they were raw and muscled and shining like a man who performs on stage. I needed memory and hope and since I could find them nowhere else, I looked for them in the declensions of verbs. Words swallowed me like a deep river. I dreamed false etymologies. I dreamed I discovered the beginning of the world in the sound of the adjective vraiment: vrai for truth and ment-ir for lie. I made new friends at the women's center, women who talked liberation and peace, women who shared sex toys and contraceptives and I liked these women and I loved walking under the poster above the women's center door that said: THE TRUTH WILL SET YOU FREE. BUT FIRST IT WILL PISS YOU OFF. I told them about you and they said, He never wrote? Forget him, there are plenty of fish in the sea.

But in a secret hour of each day I studied Khmer. The language of love. A curling script with soundless buried r's, beautifully balanced between consonants and vowels with two sounds each. I wrapped my tongue around the language of your childhood, embraced you with each new word. My teacher had a wooden leg. His name was Vithu and I paid him with my flower money. He had managed to escape across the border early in the war but not before he stepped on a landmine. He had been precocious, a farmer's son who learned to read and write at the monastery. He taught me words and he taught me how to speak. He tried to teach me modesty. He said, If someone says, You cook well or you speak well, you must say, No I don't, and lower your eyes. In Cambodia a virtuous woman moves without making a sound on the floor.

I loved the folk wisdom called chbap. Vithu taught me: Don't let a hungry man guard rice, don't let an angry man wash dishes. He taught me about khmoc, ghosts, and pret and besach, the demon spirits of people who die violent deaths and about arak, bad female spirits, and neak ta, the spirits in stones and trees. Over the years I became quite good and one day after reading aloud a story about a rabbit and a judge, I looked up to see Vithu's eyes full of tears. I touched his hand and said, You miss home very much. But he said, It is not that so much, Anne Greves; it is more that the things I have taught you are things that have surely disappeared from my home.

I told him my father could make him a better leg but he stroked his, said, I'm used to this one. One day he asked me to write my favorite Khmer story. I wrote about a king in the time Nokor Pearean Sei whose name was mighty as thunder from eight directions. His grandson wished to surpass his grandfather and destroyed everything his grandfather achieved, the royal fortresses and temples, monasteries and schools. By the time the grandson was finished, it was as if the great empire of his grandfather had never existed.

When Vithu showed me his corrections, he brushed his hand over my paper as if it too were a vanished monument and he said, In Buddhism we believe we can see ourselves in the other. Do you know the story of the rabbit in the moon? Before the Buddha was the Buddha he was a rabbit. He wanted to be reborn as the Buddha and so he offered to sacrifice his life to anyone in need. One day a tevada-angel turned himself into a starving hunter to test the rabbit. He said, I am so hungry. If I do not eat soon I will die. The rabbit said, I will sacrifice my life to help you. Make a fire and I will jump in and cook myself for you. The hunter agreed and built a blazing fire. The rabbit jumped into the flames but he was unharmed. Then the tevada carried the rabbit to the moon and drew his image there to remind people always of the Buddha's selfless kindness.

When Vithu finished he said, My sister's name was Channary, which means a girl with a face like the moon.

Where is your sister now?

Gone, he said.

14

One day walking down Bleury Street I saw FOR RENT written on a piece of cardboard taped to the window of your old apartment. I called the landlord and said, I'll take it.

There had been years of tenants since you. I ran up the long dark staircase and opened the door and wandered through the large rooms. I sniffed the closets, sat on the balcony, paced the floor in the kitchen, stood in the bedroom where I had listened over and over to "Sugarcane Baby." Every room had been painted. There were scattered images and ghosts, but not yours. I could smell Gouda cheese, and hear the laughter of six women students planning a party, and I felt the presence of a boy studying weather. I moved my bed into your old room at the front and painted it yellow again.

I was not unaffected by the liberties of the times, music and drugs and separatism. At the wild Laval dances they sometimes still played Patti Labelle singing "Lady Marmalade." I took lovers. When I visited Berthe she said tenderly, Enjoy this time, life is short, mon chou. I watched the city awkwardly absorbing Algerians and South Africans and Persians and Koreans and Chinese and Senegalese and Haitians. I searched out the places French Canadians and the children of European immigrants and the old-wealth Anglo Westmounters rarely went. I danced to reggae and disco and Haitian music in a press of warm bodies in le bar Port au Prince. One night I took home a cheerful young man who made me laugh when he said he wanted to call the book he was writing *Comment faire l'amour avec un nègre sans se fatiguer*. In the kitchen at Bleury Street we danced again. We got up from the linoleum floor ravenous and made thick milkshakes and toast and then we tried the bed. It was Sunday morning and then Sunday afternoon and in the twilight leading toward the third day, he told me he wanted to write about his grandmother in the highlands of Haiti. After he left I never saw him again and I did not mind. Longing for you, I learned, borng samlanh, that once in a lifetime, if we are lucky, we meet the one who teaches us how even fickle Eros can set free abiding love.

Then one night, eleven years after you left, I turned on the television and the light flickered in front of me. I moved my chair very close to the screen. Australian backpackers were taking a train into Phnom Penh to attend a memorial day, the Day to Remain Tied in Anger. The Vietnamese were withdrawing and the United Nations was creating a transitional government. I had watched newsreels of war and landmine victims and the hollow desperation of hunger and piles of skulls but I had never seen pictures of Cambodia trying to recover. I watched a weeping woman dressed in white behind the microphone speaking to a large crowd in the courtyard of a school that had been used as an extermination center. She was thin and she held a wet handkerchief. Her nasal voice flayed the upturned faces of the listening people. She chanted the names of her parents, her husband, her children, her brothers and sisters, taken from her one by one. Tears streamed down her face, deep lines deepening between her brows. When she paused to breathe past the lumps in her throat, she covered her face with a white handkerchief dripping tears and sweat.

Behold grief.

Words and weeping one sound. She covered her mouth with dread grace, swaying from the waist, her long fingers rippling like stalks of grain. She sang:

> *What sorrow is there that is not mine?*
> *Country lost and husband and children.*
> *What sorrow is not mine?*

Face after face after face turned away, eyes dropping, tears falling. Another young woman took her turn at the microphone and from her throat spilled a song seared with hatred. Her eyes flamed black. She was blood and tissue drained of love. She sang, *Mother, what did they do to you here?*

The monks say, Mean ruup mean dtuk. With a body comes suffering.

I saw you.

The camera panned the crowd and I was sure I saw you in the crowd.

My longing did not seem a lover's insanity in this city of the bereaved. Every person in that crowd was grieving. Nothing seemed crazy in the paralyzed longing of that crowd.

Blood pooled behind my eyes in the moment of blindness I always suffered when I looked at your photo. I was sure I had seen you alive and moving in the crowd and I could no longer pretend. I turned off the television. I packed things. I put away the picture of my mother. I gave notice at Bleury Street and the university and I went to the passport office. I got a visa. On Sunday night I told Papa I was leaving in two days and he shook his head. He said, You have not heard from him in a decade. You *think* you saw him on television. You are quitting your job before the term is finished? What the hell. Why can't you wait?

We sat in silence. The food tasted like dust. He set down his fork and said, You are ruining your life.

I said, I did not want to leave without saying good-bye.

He stared at the table in silence. After a long time he looked at me as if I were a ghost, It is your life. Your mother was like this too. She too gave up everything.

He reached out to touch my cheek, said as if to himself, If you find him I may never see you again.

I laughed, cleared the table and said, Papa, do not be so dramatic.

But he insisted, There are things you do not know.

15

I took my money from the bank and bought an airline ticket. To Paris. To Phnom Penh. We arrived after dawn and I hired a taxi to take me from Pochentong Airport down the highway toward the city. I remember the heat. The roofs, blues and greens and corrugated tin and thick plastic and red tiles. Golden spires from the palace by the river and the graceful curves of the wat on the Phnom Penh hill above the clutter of markets and apartments and huts and animals. Along the roadside, people set up stalls under umbrellas and awnings, cooked food in steaming pots, sold sweet drinks from orange and white coolers. Women without shoes carried their babies in cloth pouches tied front and back, watched toddlers with bare bottoms and staring eyes and fingers in their mouths. The taxi turned deeper into the narrowing streets, drove toward the river into city blocks with rounded buildings that looked like Paris, past the downtown street markets and into a neighborhood of apartments with airy wide terraces on upper floors. The driver stopped in front of your family's house, Phlauv 350, and I got out and paid him too many American dollars and stood on the street feeling the heat and my heart beating. I wondered if you would answer the door.

I knocked. A young woman holding a baby cracked it open and I was breaking. She said firmly, No. No he does not live here. That family has never lived here. Then she looked at my face and said kindly, Maybe they lived here before. I think I have heard their name.

She closed the door and, exhausted from the long flight, from the heat of Phnom Penh, I thought, What have I done?

An old woman squatted on the sidewalk next door watching me. I approached her and asked, The family that lived there before, did you know them?

She said, You speak good Khmer.

Not so good, I said, but I had a good teacher. Do you know the family who used to live there?

The skin around the corner of her left eye tightened and the eye twitched. She said, There were two brothers; they played with my children. Gone, they are all gone.

I squatted beside her in the doorway. I called her Yay, the word for grandmother.

I am looking for the older brother. Did you ever see him? I think he must have come here.

She studied my eyes and said, He used to come here but I have not seen him for many years. No one else came back.

She looked down the street of ghosts and said, I lost my whole family during Pol Pot.

I did not know what to say. A baby cried inside, behind the shutters. I asked, What can I do?

She answered, I only want you to know.

I will come back and see you, Yay. When I find him I will tell him I met you.

Her neck twitched. Yes, tell him you saw Chan. I will be here.

This was my first day in Phnom Penh, the day I met Mau.

Phnom Penh

16

When Mau stepped forward the other drivers fell back. He listened, assessing and calculating, when I told him that I wanted to look for you in all the nightclubs of Phnom Penh. He showed me his remorque with a yellow fringe in the busy market. He was a small man with a scar on his left cheek. He wore a Chicago Cubs baseball cap. His eyes softened fleetingly when he looked at me and he said, Maybe it will take time, maybe it is like looking for a single grain of rice.

I was not sure how I would find you and I was not sure you wanted me to. The smell of the River Bassac, meltwaters from distant mountains tangled into humid air and garlic and night jasmine and cooking oil and male sweat and female wetness. Corruption loves the darkness. In Montreal I knew which doors, which alleys, which snowbanks hid bags of drugs and young girls with red lips and skinny boys with narrow hips, the things men think they want. But here I did not know where anything was and I was afraid to go out alone to look for you.

Mau pulled into traffic, and I was relieved to be out of the crowds of the market. Everyone trying to make a few riel. Mau stopped in front of Lucky No. 1 Restaurant on Monivong Boulevard and called to a waiter to give me a table on the sidewalk. I asked Mau to eat soup with me but he waved his hand in front of his face. He said, I must watch my moto. I will wait.

Families sat in doorways trying to escape the heat. Men on the street took note of me with casual, calculating eyes: a white woman alone with dollars somewhere on her. A bicycle rolled in front of my table and the front wheel crushed the back of a rat. It writhed in ragged circles. Two waiters tried to nudge it away from my table with the tips of their rubber flip-flops but they were afraid. Finally they got a broom and swept the dying rat into a bucket and threw it still alive and twisting into a bin in the alley.

The Heart was packed and you were not there. I did not expect to find you in the first place I looked. But I hoped. I looked into the shine of eyes that did not recognize me and stepped back out the door. Mau pulled up and said, I know another place. He drove around Independence Monument to a small club called Nexus. A DJ sat behind a rickety table playing a collection of jazz records on a turntable and Khmer music on a cassette player. This was a place you might be. Very pre-genocide. But you were not here. I came out and said to Mau, What if he has a girlfriend?

Night after night Mau drove me. We crossed the river to restaurants packed with beer girls and men reaching for them and I said, He would not be here. Mau shrugged as if to say, All things are possible. It was April, almost New Year's, the hottest time of the year, and the clubs and bars were full every night. I thought, What if he does not go out to listen to music anymore? What if I never go to the same place at the same time? What if the gods are deaf and mute and play tricks on me forever?

In the mornings I walked on Sisowath Quay, watched the traffic, an oxcart piled with wood and big bunches of bananas tied to the outside rail, a bicycle with a slaughtered hog, eyes open, tongue out, lashed on crosswise, small cars and motorcycles making Phnom Penh merges, cutting diagonally across oncoming traffic. On the wide sidewalks people carried large flat baskets filled with fruit and greens on their heads, carried little stools to sit on. Every morning a man without legs drove a bicycle with hand-pedals along the river path eastward. I found Sopheap's noodle cart. She carried a baby tied to her back and a toddler played near her feet. I watched her face through the steam of her boiling pot and I liked the graceful way she stirred the noodles and her gentleness with the child and I approached her and said in Khmer, A bowl of noodles please with sait moan.

She said, You speak good Khmer.

No, just a little.

She lifted hot noodles from the pot into a chipped bowl, spooned out some meat and handed it to me.

Men in long-sleeved white shirts strolled on the quay in the brief cool of dawn, buying and selling. People jostled at a cart across the street selling pomelos. Whoever had money could eat hot rice and noodles, sugarcane, squid, boiled eggs, lotus root from the carts. Baskets of fried grasshoppers, later trays of ice cream. Hungry children reached out thin hands on the sidewalks. Food. Cigarettes. Petrol. Boys. Girls. Tourists. Traffic police waved people over for license checks. Demanded bribes. Drivers made U-turns as soon as they saw the police. People without arms and legs moved in the shadows of doorways, begging, sleeves turned up and neatly pinned over stumps of arms, harder to beg without arms, a few lucky ones on metal legs, or maybe a heaven-sent three-wheeled bicycle.

I handed Sopheap my empty bowl, said, Juab kh'nia th'ngay krao-y.

She smiled, Have you been here long?

A few days.

How did you learn to speak Khmer?

I studied at home. It is the language of my ...

I searched for a word. I knew how to say brother, father, husband, but I had never learned a word for lover.

It is the language of the man I love, I said. I am looking for him.

It was ordinary that people were missing in this place. As ordinary as missing an arm or a leg.

Sopheap smiled her radiant smile and said, I hope you find him. Tell me what he looks like and I will watch for him. I see many people every day.

After that I went each morning for breakfast at Sopheap's cart. She told me she was young during Pol Pot and her mother had managed to keep her but that her older brothers died and her father died. She met her husband in a refugee camp on the Thai border. Her mother had wanted to take her abroad but they were not accepted. And so they came back.

In the afternoons I went to the Foreign Correspondents' Club. I liked the Parisian yellow bricks, the thwuck thwuck of the ceiling fans, the clean tablecloths, the stools at an open bar looking over the river and boulevard, colonial decadence. A Westerner arrives with a few dollars and lives like royalty and this unheard-of wealth is the first thing I shared with the foreigners at the FCC. Here I did not have to be lonely. Here someone was always telling stories. Here was rest from struggle on the streets. Among journalists and foreign aid workers and UN workers and backpackers, among the deliberate wanderers of the earth, there was no need to explain looking for a lost lover. Backpackers talked about bars and dope in Thailand, beaches in India, cathedrals in Europe, their mothers. They drifted through Phnom Penh, explored sex and skulls and temples, talked about going to the beaches in the south for New Year's. Down on the street, children tossed chestnuts in a game called angkunh, and people decorated their tables and stores for the holidays with lotus flowers. From the rooftop of the FCC I looked in one direction over the palace and imagined what it must have been like to live in royal opulence, to attend orange and gold Buddhist processions, to celebrate the plowing on the full moon, and in the other direction I watched ordinary people on their terraces, a woman slaughtering a chicken for dinner, a teenager nursing her baby in a hammock.

17

On New Year's Day the FCC was quiet. Most people had been invited somewhere or visited the temples to thank the old year's angels, to welcome new angels. A man I had often seen came through the door. He was very tall with wide shoulders and a bit of a belly, strong forearms, sun-darkened skin. His brown eyes took detail in, and I had noticed him watching me. He bought a beer, came over and slid onto a stool beside me at the empty bar looking over the street. He said, Can I join you? It's crowded in here.

From the beginning Will Maracle made me laugh.

I'm Will.

I'm Anne Greves.

He said, I see you here every afternoon.

I know.

Happy New Year.

And to you.

He set his glass down where it sweated a ring of water and said, What are you doing here?

I am looking for my lover.

Are you American?

I'm from Montreal.

Me too, near Montreal. Funny New Year's without snow.

Funny New Year's in April.

He flickered with a sweet light. There was a rhythm in his English I could not place. I asked, Where near Montreal?

Kahnawake.

That's Montreal.

No it ain't. It's on the other side of the river.

He laughed his easy laugh and said, Why on god's green earth are you looking for your lover here? And why would he lose someone as pretty as you?

I took a drink and said, What are you doing so far from home?

Forensics.

I looked at him.

Counting.

Counting?

They are trying to figure out how many.

Will Maracle opened massacre sites, released the bones. We talked all afternoon. I asked him what Maracle meant and he didn't know. He asked me what Greves meant and I told him it was a whaler's word, the refuse of tallow. I told him about looking for you in all the bars of the city. We talked about French and English and how he got started digging Indian burial grounds, trained with a man named Clyde Snow in Argentina and ended here. I asked him how he could bear his work and he said, Truth is as old as God. He shrugged and said, Someone else said that, not me.

I answered, And will endure as long as He, A Co-Eternity.

Will laughed.

It must be hard work, I said.

It is not shards of pottery. I like the intuition it takes to get bones together, to make sense of the scene. It is human work. Anyway, I'm used to it.

His eyes drifted away and he said, Sometimes I have this dream about severed legs in bed with me. Then he looked back and said, You are a good listener.

Sometimes. Where are you working now?

I'm fucking the dog. Things stop and start. There's no political will. The leaders don't want to know. But I like it here.

An elephant swayed up the street. Thin holiday traffic separated around it. I told him I got up at dawn to watch a Mountain and Sand ceremony, five piles of sand in the temple courtyard, the five footsteps of the Buddha, and the monks planted rice sticks decorated with colored paper in the piles and lit incense sticks and sprinkled the sand mountains with scented water.

Will said, I have heard you speaking Khmer. You are lucky. You know what is going on.

We fell silent, listened to each other's breath.

Will said, Want to go see the Buddha get bathed?

What's that?

He took my hand and pulled me off the bar stool, said, Too depressing sitting here alone on New Year's. Let's go. I'm meeting some people.

We walked to a small neighborhood temple near a massage room called Seeing Hands, a workplace for landmine victims. An old woman who had lost a leg at the knee waited on a wooden chair beside a young woman with a face that shocked me. She had no eyes and no nose. The center of her face was a rectangle of shiny skin graft. The skin on her forehead, above the graft, was moist and young. A hole near the center of the graft had been constructed as a nostril. Below the graft her lips were sensual and full and she had a delicate chin and a beautiful neck.

Will touched her hand, said, Sineth, I brought along a friend, Anne Greves. She speaks Khmer.

She smiled with those full round lips and reached her hand gracefully toward me. In English she said, Hello. This my friend Bopha. We go now?

She stood and took Will's arm and walked beside him down the three steps. In the courtyard of the temple a few monks and some elders and a scatter of people. People sprinkled consecrated water on the elders and monks. Sineth explained they were asking forgiveness for any mistakes they had made and promising to make the elders happy in the coming year. I translated for Will, then Bopha said where she came from in the north at New Year's there was a coconut dance for the young people. Suddenly a middle-aged man poured a jug of water on a man beside him and everyone laughed and splashed water at each other and the monks withdrew. Sineth smiled at the sounds and whispered, When I was young, this ceremony was much bigger, everyone got wet. I used to go with my sister and mother and father and brothers.

Later, walking on the quay, I asked Will, What happened to Sineth?

He said, A pan of acid. Jealous boyfriend. Crazy fuck. In another world I would ask a girl with lips like that to dance with me.

I said, Why not? Why not fall in love with her lips?

I wish it were so simple.

We watched fireworks on the quay and walked past carts selling sweets and cigarettes and fruit and noodles. Will stared at the river, said, I'll make a New Year's wish for you. I hope you find who you are looking for. And I'll make a wish for me. I hope they start work again, so I can stay.

How long have you been here?

Long enough to fall in love with it.

His face was calm in the reflection of firelight off the water. I said, I hope your wish comes true. I cannot imagine what it is like to open a grave.

Will said, These are old graves. It is easier than fresh ones.

Two small boys ran past and tossed firecrackers at our feet. We jumped aside laughing, turned up a dark street. I asked, Once we know, what do we do?

Fireworks made with gold and silver paint exploded, drifted like milkweed seeds across the black sky. Will said, Maybe the only hope is that our humanity might kick into a higher gear, that the more we admit to seeing, the more we will believe we are not that different from each other.

18

Imagine a street; imagine waking up one morning and teenaged voices outside shouting, Comrades, it is Year Zero.

Country kids who cannot drive lurch down the street in tanks and trucks. They have been hiding out in the jungle. They screech brakes, pop clutches. They scream through megaphones. They fire guns and kill anyone who talks back or asks questions or, god forbid, refuses to move. They do not have good judgment. But they can choose anyone to die. Most neither read nor write. Imagine going out into the street and watching a man ask why he must leave his home and a teenager lifting his gun and shooting him.

Think of the old mother who cannot walk. Her children cannot get to her. These hard-eyed boy-soldiers dressed in loose black pants and shirts tramp through the hospital and shoot anyone who cannot get up. Think of people trying to push hospital beds along the road.

Imagine the walk out of the city. People do not know where they will sleep. There is no clean water. Nowhere to shit. No one knows what to bring. Does anyone have matches? A cooking pot? A cup? Old people die on the roadside and people walk past them because soldiers are waving guns. A woman gives birth in a ditch. City people become thirsty, crouching creatures. Hunger makes their heads throb. Mothers snap at their children. People steal bowls from corpses. What else can they do? What is a person capable of?

Year Zero. The country has a new name. Everyone works on farms. Seed. Plant. Harvest with knives. Pound. Winnow. Bag for the soldiers.

Music is forbidden. Talk is forbidden.

The soldiers make bonfires of libraries and paper money. Everyone is hungry.

Banks. Gone.

Mail. Gone.

Telephones. Gone.

Radio. Gone.

Teenagers serve Angka, the Organization. The leader is Brother Number One. No one knows yet his name is Pol Pot. No one knows he used to be a schoolteacher called Saloth Sar. How did this happen? People fell asleep and when they woke up nothing was the same. Would a person risk helping a neighbor if a nervous, shouting teenager were pointing a gun?

In Year Zero there is no past.

19

I walked into the Globe on Sihanouk Boulevard and I saw you standing at the bar. Your dark hair was still long, tied back, and you wore a white T-shirt. You leaned on the bar and you were alone and absorbed in the music. You. In Phnom Penh. *Where you go, I will go.* And your eyes. Gold flecked. Mud dark. Blood gathered behind my eyes and the room went black and I blinked and breathed and saw you again.

The DJ put on an old Oscar Peterson recording. I listened to that caressing, flirting, demanding touch on a piano playing "L'impossible." Now that I had found you I had to get used to you again. When the song was finished you shifted on your feet and looked around, and your eyes passed over me and then I watched them flicker back startled and rest on me. *Where you lodge, I will lodge.* And then you were walking away from the bar, your arms lifting and you were taller than I remembered, still wiry and slender, the skin of your face not so translucent, and I loved all over again that chipped-tooth smile. *Where you die, I will die, and there will I be buried.* Your fingers touched my shoulders and light shone like stars at the center of your eyes and I said to you in Khmer, I found you. I felt your arms hard around me and I smelled the smell of you, as if we were animals.

I was sixteen years old standing in the bite of cold air under the light of a cross on a snowy mountain and I was an old woman who remembers the night I found you in the beer and cigarette smell of Phnom Penh. You were the one I fell in love with and you were someone who lost everyone in this place where ghosts haunt the grieving and the corrupt and I felt something catch in you, a sob or a startle, and light drenched the dark room.

I was not afraid anymore and I would not have to search through dark bars alone anymore and I ran out to tell Mau and I was laughing the way I used to before my laughter hid things, before I lost love.

Sometimes with an old lover there is a fleeting sensation of the disappointment of flesh. But I felt none. I felt the infinite attentiveness that is love.

Do you know me?

I know your eyes.

You reached out and touched my hair, said, How did you find me?

I don't know.

How long have you been here?

I am not sure.

Where are you staying?

With you.

And then you smiled again. You said, Now I know it is you, Anne Greves. Suddenly you stopped and said, You are speaking Khmer. *And your people shall be my people and your God, my God.*

20

Mau told me months later, Borng srei, after we found him and I saw him go away with you on his own moto with the sidecar, I went home. I did not want to drive foreigners anymore that night. I wanted to go home and sleep until morning beside Ary because I had not done this with her for a long time.

21

Phnom Penh. The leisurely put-put sway to the traffic, rickshaws drawn by skinny barefoot men who run or pedal bicycles, four-wheeled remorques drawn by motorcycles, white UN vans, Red Cross trucks, military jeeps and buses, an elephant carrying lumber, the streets wrinkling up from the waterfront, Street 51 hits a dead end at Street 392 and intersects 254, everything patched together without logic, like family love. And signs along the street for all kinds of English, Practical English, Office English, Business English, Streamline English. White-shirted students walk in small groups, and whole families move home for the night on a motorbike, always the man driving and the wife holding a baby and a grandmother holding a toddler, and once in a blue moon a woman damaged by beating or acid running naked and crazed into the streets.

And so, in Phnom Penh among the beggars and amputees and prostitutes and street children, in the midst of all that relentless struggle, we were together again. Truly the darkness is sweet in Cambodia.

Your stark room. The street noise, the night pressing against wide shutters. I touched your tidy table. I sat on the edge of the bed. It would take only a few minutes to pack up and disappear. For years you had lived in barren order. The picture of your family was tacked up near the table. The two photo booth pictures of us were tacked near the bed. A large fan thwucked on the ceiling. You still used the same cassette player and you had fixed two shelves above your table, one with a few books in Khmer and one lined with little cassette boxes of pirated music. Your old chapei was wrapped in a bit of cloth in the corner. My presence took up so much space. What did I expect? A sprawling tropical home, family, girlfriend, rhythmic ceiling fans over teak tables and built-in library with books in many languages?

I asked, Your family?

You said, Why did you never answer my letters?

What letters?

You said, There is too much. Later. We will talk more later.

The body remembers. I opened myself to you as if I could be unzipped front and back. In the first moments you touched me as an unknown territory, slowly, remembering a softness I think you had forgotten. Your arms, the taste of your skin, your eyes. I could hardly breathe. I received your touch, you received my relief as if we were giving agonized birth to each other. But I could not stay shy, I wanted you, I had wanted you for eleven years and we became cannibals swallowing flesh and breathing prayers. I was not shy, and even if I could have you only this one night I did not care.

After, combing your fingers through my hair, you said, I am happy for the first time since I left you. This is the truth. And then with your charming smile, Anne Greves, I am starving.

I said, I know.

The print of each other's hands and mouths still on our skin, we went to a restaurant to eat phnom pleung, turning bits of fish over the small barbecue on the table, famished, and we ate green morning glory stems with rice. We could not stop looking, touching each other now with our eyes. A child came by with an armful of pkaa malis and you bought all her strings of flowers and gave them to me, and the child ran smiling back to a man slouching on the corner. I lifted the jasmine to my nose and you said, It is a full moon day. Do not smell them yet, bad luck. Bring them home to offer to the house spirits.

Under the table our feet touched. A waiter checked the flame and you spoke to him so rapidly I could not understand and the waiter went away.

You said, I see snow on your eyelashes. And I hear French and English. I am listening to Buddy Guy. But I am no longer with a girl. You are different now, stronger.

I said, People do not really change; we are only undefeated because we have gone on trying.

You smiled, said, Maybe they do change, little tiger.

I did not know yet how you had changed. I asked, What do you do?

Translation.

I said, Your studies abroad were useful.

You took my hand on the table, said, More useful than for languages, oan samlanh.

And I knew I would stay with you forever.

We ate slowly and the waiter returned with a little leaf parcel secured with a piece of toothpick. You put it in my hand, This is pkaa champa, for you.

A scent like magnolia from three delicate buds wrapped in a leaf. I resisted putting them to my nose.

The old poets rarely describe requited love. How can they resist?

Did you have lovers? You were first to ask.

I have only ever loved you.

Already we were wandering hand in hand to leave the garden. I said, And you? You must have had many lovers.

None.

We told each other these falsehoods of love and fetched my bag from my empty guest room and brought it back to your room, which smelled now of jasmine and magnolia, and after we made love you slept and dreamed, frantic eyes darting back and forth under closed lids, and when you opened your eyes again, I said, Tell me.

I do not want you to have to know. In my dreams Sokha accuses me. My parents are behind him staring at me from big silent eyes. But my younger brother stands in front of me and says over and over, Why did you do nothing?

22

You were shocked, at first, by what you saw, a skeleton-people struggling numbly back into the silent city. A family had already taken over your old family home. Numb, you found this room on Sisowath Quay. The first silence of the city was broken by foreign aid trucks rumbling back and forth and the shouts of Vietnamese soldiers. At odd moments on the street two people would suddenly recognize each other and burst into little islands of talk, sifting through memories of who they had last seen where, who had died when. They stood in the street, sometimes holding each other, then weeping and talking, relief at finding anyone alive, telling how they survived, each tear like a small match thrown into a barrel of gasoline. The first year there was little planting as people struggled slowly home all across the country. Then followed two years of famine. When the foreign relief workers arrived and no one knew Khmer you had endless work translating.

You said, All through Pol Pot time people could not speak freely. Neighbor against neighbor. Children trained to report on their families. People tried to hide inside the same skin. People pretended not to be city people, pretended not to understand foreign languages, tried to disguise soft hands, tried to pass as farmers, taxi drivers, street vendors.

Who did you find? Did you find Tien?

Musicians were the enemy. Students were the enemy. City people and educated people. Everything I had been was the enemy.

A soul protects itself from what it cannot bear. You would not speak of your family. You said, But I found a new chapei teacher. Some people survived.

You got up then and took your chapei from the corner of the room and unwrapped it. You sat on the bed cross legged and you lay the instrument across your lap and plucked the two strings. You sang an old folk song about yearning for the time of the monsoon winds, oan samlanh, yearning to go to the festival with your love, wearing a new phamuong, oh dear one, going together to the festival with your love.

You looked at me to see if I still liked your singing.

When you first got back you walked across the city to your old street, past your old front door looking for your family. Nothing. You went to the Red Cross center with their lists of names. Nothing.

I met Chan, I said.

You went to my home?

Yes. It was the first place I looked.

You said, The country was like a shattered slate. Before they could think of drawing lines on it, they had to find the pieces and fit them together again.

You pulled open a drawer and took out a school notebook and flipped through it to show me pages of lyrics written in your precise Khmer script.

I have been learning the old songs, you said. I know many more than when I knew you. I have broken with tradition by writing them down.

Then you closed the book and put it back in the drawer and you took me in your arms and said, It seems like a dream, you here.

Dawn light soon filled the lines between the shutters and I did not want daylight and heat. We lay in bed touching, whispering.

What did you do?

I did not tell you the pain of receiving no word. I did not tell you how I wondered if a human being can invent love. I did not tell you how I began to notice that people marry every day not for love but because they are well matched, or lonely.

I said, At first I tried to telephone you but it was impossible. I sent letters to Phlauv 350. I studied and later I taught.

Your eyes were so alive. I laughed and said, I rented your old apartment. I painted the bedroom yellow again. For years I tried to tell myself that it was over. But a few weeks ago, I saw you on television. It was a ceremony for the dead at a school here. I thought I saw you in the crowd.

You said, I never go to those ceremonies.

I laughed, Then there was no reason to come at all.

I pretended to get up to leave but you pulled me back and I was happy that you could still play.

I said, The night after I thought I saw you, there was a late spring snowstorm. I walked from Bleury Street up past the Yellow Door and past La Bodega, where I tasted my first sangria with you and near the pub where you sang. I climbed past the university to the top of the mountain, where we argued about you leaving, and then I walked toward St. Joseph's. Do you remember how we watched the people climbing the steps on their knees? I did not want to go home and I walked all the way to the train station past Marie-Reine-du-Monde. I was tired but I kept walking, to old Montreal, past L'air du temps and I remembered Sonny and Brownie. Finally I went home. The whole city and every step reminded me of you.

A single tear slipped along the side of your nose and you brushed it away. You said, Let's go out for a walk.

I said, No, wait. Tell me what happened to your family.

What I know belongs to another person, you said. Better to shut it away in a closed box. Let's go out.

I followed you. Of course. We crossed the street to the wide promenade by the river. I saw Sopheap's noodle cart and we stopped for noodles and when she saw you her eyes sparkled and she asked, Is it him?

I nodded and she laughed and handed us two bowls of noodles, said, No money today. Today is a celebration.

After we finished eating we walked along the river in the gathering heat of morning and you said, Who else do you already know here? I forgot how free you are.

We walked in front of the Royal Palace and you said, Have you visited yet? We passed through the Chan Chaya Pavilion where the dancers once performed, up the marble staircase and over the silver tiles of the Pagoda of the Emerald Buddha. We looked at the Emerald Buddha made of Baccarat crystal and the gold Buddha encrusted with diamonds and a small silver and gold stupa that contained a relic of the Buddha from Sri Lanka. I liked best the standing Burmese Buddha made of marble, and you showed me the library of sacred texts inscribed on palm leaves. We watched two children playing a game like tic-tac-toe in the sand and looked at the golden roofs of the palace with their flame-shaped peaks and naga snakes and bright blue mosaics and we watched geckos darting under enormous urns planted with palms. You said, Remember how we visited all the churches of Montreal? We walked back to a sidewalk café below the FCC and drank strong Italian coffee and we talked about eleven years of days, and restless, you said, Let's go listen to music.

23

I thought we were going to a café but instead I followed you to a squatter camp called Dey Krohom. You bought a sack of rice in one of the markets. Rows of huts of corrugated metal and plastic sheeting and woven rattan. Broken coconut husks on the ground. The smell of charcoal and wood fire. You led me through the narrow paths to a house where a man with pocked skin lay dozing on a kgrair behind a pair of black sunglasses. You called softly, Uncle, it is me, and you placed the rice under his wooden slatted bed.

His face was instantly cut in two by a wide smile and as he sat up, you leaned into my hair and joked in English, Meet Ray Charles, but to him you said in respectful Khmer, Teacher Kong Nai, I have brought a friend who likes your music. You put my hand in his. Nai smiled at me and squeezed my hand in his warm palm. You said, Would you play? and he called back into the house to a young woman who brought out his old instrument. He tucked his legs sideways under him and played and sang stories of giants and harvest and he sang his own name. Two little girls appeared from the outside edge of his home and danced, wrists bent back, graceful fingers spread, and adults slipped away from their cooking fires to listen. Kong Nai felt his wife approach and turned toward her with that luminous smile. He played the music that I had heard on your cassette tapes in the room on Bleury Street, the bluesy moan of strings and human voice. You glanced at me and studied the master's fingers and looked at the small crowd of people listening.

Most of the musicians were dead and most of the dancers were dead and most of the painters were dead. Some who lived hid themselves away and drank. Some had pretended to be mad to survive and could not fully shed their pretended madness. Some said, Better artists than I were killed, but they found the strength to keep working. When Nai finished, he said to me, Come any time. I like to play.

We walked out through the narrow pathways and you said, Nai is the one I wanted to bring to L'air du temps.

Salt sweat and wood smoke and the river. The light of little fires, the smell of cooking rice and frying fish. The darkness of a city still unlit.

How did he survive?

He harvested corn and beans. He made palm rope. He sang revolutionary songs. By the end, he too was on their lists.

24

You wrote to me. One blue aerogram once a week. When you told me, I thought over and over and over and over, How could Papa have done this to me?

I said, How long did you keep writing?

I sent you a letter last week. The letters never came back. They were going somewhere. I thought that one might get through. Sometimes I thought nothing. I just wrote.

Why didn't you phone?

Oan samlanh, I did, once. Your father answered and said, Do not call again. She has someone else.

Betrayed. In the name of love my father kept you from me and still I found you. I did not read your words that told, now that you were gone, your undying love.

People keep secrets from each other all the time. People hide lovers. Women hide babies. Parents hide their weakness from their children. Children hide who they are from their parents. Who do we degrade with our secrets?

Why do we long for love in abandon? Love that cannot endure. The world is outside the garden. We cover our bodies and keep living and hope until the end for love in abandon. One more time.

25

After a few days your telephone rang in the morning.

You answered, Hallo? ... Baat ... baat ... Baan ... Okay, bye.

When you hung up you said, I should go back to work.

And so our days settled into an easy rhythm. Early each morning you went out to work and returned in the mid afternoon. I wandered through the city, the markets, the small alleys, the temples. I visited Chan in your old neighborhood. I talked with Sopheap. I found the taxi stand where Mau started each day before dawn. When it was very hot I went to the pool at the Cambodiana hotel and swam and watched the foreigners. You said you were a translator and I believed you. You would not speak of your family. I trusted you. I reasoned, There has been great pain. When the telephone rang, the only intrusion in our room, you said you were making work appointments and of course I believed you.

You would hang up and say, I will be back early today, about two o'clock, oan samlanh. Tonight we should go to the Globe. Listen to music. See you later.

Domestic talk. More exotic than lovers' talk, I had lived so long alone. I loved your casual pledge each time you left, See you later. I did not ask for more. I did not ask where you worked or who you worked for. I thought, We have forever. I have waited this long. In the cool late afternoons we made love and in the evenings we roamed the city on foot or on your motor-bike with the sidecar. You were often silent. But you still liked to play music and you learned again to joke with me. We ate at carts and sat on benches looking over the river and I told you about our old friends in Montreal, how Charlotte married and had three children, how No Exit found another lead, then drifted away from music to offices and marriages and babies; you told me about traveling north to your grandparents' village and finding a friend.

One morning I said, I want to go to Choeung Ek. Will you drive me this afternoon? I want to see the killing fields.

You said, Why go to Choeung Ek? You already know what happened.

I want to see for myself. Come with me. I want to know what you know.

Your face closed and you said, No need to see. You already know.

But I want to see.

No need, little tiger.

After you left I walked across the city to Psar Tuol Tom Pong, the Russian market, and I found Mau and asked him to drive me.

We discarded the city at the fork in the road that leads to the old longan orchard. The fields were grown over with grass, and a stupa in the killing fields sheltered eight thousand skulls.

In Choeung Ek memory flips its dark belly to the surface like a water beetle hiding in plain view. Depressions in the earth overgrown with grass. Stupas of skulls and bones. The sky. A young man neatly dressed in a clean shirt and light cotton pants approached Mau and me. His eyes were so flat that I could not bear to look into them and he said, I will tell you what happened.

We sat with him and he said, I saw with my own eyes how they killed. In my work brigade they called a big meeting. They dragged out a young couple and blindfolded them and tied them to a tree. They ordered my brigade to come and see people who fall in love without permission from Angka.

What should we do? the leaders yelled.

My brigade yelled back, Kill! Kill!

I yelled this thing too. The boy beside me stepped forward with a bamboo stick and hit the man across his head. Blood came out of his nose and his ears and his eyes. They took the blindfold off the woman and she went pale and she closed her eyes and they beat her too. After many blows they finished her off. I did this thing too. I hit a still living human being hard on the head and the neck and stomach.

Why did you shout, Kill, kill?

He moved his hands in circles in front of his chest and he said, I did not feel anything at that time. Words came out with all the other voices.

The Khmer Rouge used words to kill the people. Touk min chom nenh dork chenh kor min kat. Sam at kmang. They said these things over and over, To keep you is no benefit, to lose you is no loss. Cleanse the enemy.

These were phrases I had never studied.

The young man raised his hands into an open funnel in front of his face and he looked through them. He said, I am a living dead. I have my body, I can move, I can speak, I can eat, but I am nothing.

Then he fell silent and Mau said, Little brother, what we think, we become.

We watched two small boys catching frogs in the gullies of the fields, running past paddy and sugar palm and cloth and bone. The grass had done its work.

We walked back to the remorque and I said to Mau, How did you survive?

He ran the key to his motorcycle over the palm of his hand. He said, Borng srei, I do not like to talk about that time. I was a fisherman's son. I pretended I could not read and I was taken to build a dam. When it was over, it was the Buddhist New Year. I joined a circle of bodies that danced and clapped around a fire under the moonlight. I myself felt finally free. Across the circle I saw the others were corpses dancing, and I looked down at my own body and it too was only skin stretched over bone. But I kept dancing. We were so happy. When we got to Phnom Penh, Ary managed to lease some land to grow mushrooms and with the profits I bought my motorcycle to make a good living. That is what happened to me.

Quietly Mau turned away. Come, borng srei, he said, you have seen enough.

When I came back, you were sitting cross legged on the bed playing your guitar and I sat near you and put my arms around you and said, Borng samlanh, today I visited Choeung Ek.

You would not speak and you did not put the guitar aside. I watched you slide your callused fingers up the neck and play a few more notes. I put my hand over your right hand so you could not play and said, I cannot live with your silence.

You still would not speak and that was the first time since we were together again that I spoke chill, impatient words I can hardly bear to remember. You are like a spirit I once knew, I said. Speak to me. Tell me what happened.

Dread stillness. After a long time you lifted your hand to touch my hair with your fingers and you reached across the guitar and pulled me to you and pressed your cheek against my head and said, You always smell so good.

Then you dropped your hands back on your guitar and smiled lightly and said, I wonder if you remember this one. You sang, *I can't get enough of your sweetness*, and I saw you on stage a long time ago, when you were still a math student from far away who could charm a crowd, but I did not sing with you.

I said, Sometimes the things that draw people together are the same things that rip them apart.

You said, Do you want to go up the river to visit the temples near where my grandparents used to live? I will show you where I come from.

26

Before the monsoons the waters were low, but still we set out in the pill-shaped Royal Express, the four-hour boat from Sisowath Quay. A television blasted Thai soap operas and music videos from Hong Kong. As soon as we were away from the docks, we climbed out the door and edged along the narrow gunwale to find a place on the roof of the boat. We tied kramas over our heads and watched villages on stilts at the river's edge. We sat shoulder against shoulder, the wind in our ears, at ease together, as if we were riding your motorcycle along the shore of the St. Lawrence. You said, You will remember this river all your life.

The Royal Express broke down and we waited on the shore for another, smaller boat, watching the children, and you talked about your grandparents' home at the phum near Angkor Wat, gibbons squabbling at dawn, chapei singers at dusk, gongs echoing through the village. You told me in a voice soft with affection that a man you played with as a boy would meet us. I looked into the gold-flecked water and I saw your eyes in the ripples.

Flocks of egrets skimmed the great lake and tall trees rose from the low water. When the prop of the small boat stuttered against the mud, we stopped again and the driver lowered himself overboard with a wrench. We moved inside to escape the blistering sun and soon the engine caught again and we pushed on through the shallow marshes as the river spread into the lake and we motored past trees growing out of the water to a floating jetty where pirogues waited and men called out prices for a poled ride to the bouncing narrow walkway on stilts above mudflats.

You called out and waved, excited, Aa-Leap! to a man in a crescent moon-shaped boat with a long rudder half eaten by the water.

We jumped into his boat and he steered us into the waterways of the floating village, rows of floating houses strapped onto oil-drum pontoons, floating shops with cigarettes and soda bottles of outboard engine oil, a floating purple clapboard school and a floating hospital clinic. It might have been a charming drawing in a child's book but for the poverty and struggle. The people of the floating village worked in bamboo-walled fish corrals, and a gray police boat with a machine gun mounted on its side was moored near a floating office marked BUREAU DE LA POLICE FLUVIALE. A small, naked boy with a wide smile spun in a floating bucket.

We glided past blue shuttered floating houses with floating porches and hanging flower pots. Leap moved us with his single rudder to a little house looking over the lake and fishing scows anchored nearby. I watched the late afternoon sun light Leap's tranquil face copper and purple.

You said to me in English, Leap's grandfather knew mine. We played together when we were children. When I first got back he saw me in my grandparents' village and said, Is it you? and I said, Are you alive?

Leap left us at a floating house as the sun disappeared and we sat on bamboo mats on the porch looking across the lake. Soon his wife appeared through a tear in the darkness squatting in the bow of his boat. She handed us hot rice wrapped in leaves and a fish steeped in coconut milk, baked in a banana leaf. We spoke about the fishing and the coming monsoons and I said, Come join us.

But she nodded to the bamboo walls and answered in a soft voice, Ears everywhere. Eyes as many as the eyes of a pineapple.

Then she disappeared again into the watery alleys of the village.

Why is she afraid to sit with us? I asked.

You joked, Maybe it's your accent.

I did not understand then that everywhere people watched each other. And sometimes they told and sometimes they did not in this place that was not free.

We ate and stowed away big bottles of water. We listened to fishing families at the end of the day, dishes and pots, card games, a baby crying, the low murmur of evening gossip. The lake was wide and very white and the people who slept with darkness and awoke before dawn fell instantly silent. All day they watched the sky and the water, read the signs of changing hours and seasons, honored the gods as naturally as they breathed, waited for the oil drums to rise again and the village to float out into the lake. Stars turned across the sky. Everything drifts and returns.

You took a tiny pink coral Buddha on a fine silver chain out of your pocket and you fastened it around my neck. I had nothing to give you but my old St. Christopher medal, which my father had given my mother and then gave me, and I undid it and put it around your neck.

We pledged ourselves to each other with our bodies. In the darkness alone together, we said that we would care for each other until death. There was no one to witness to us and so we were witnessed only by the nameless missing and by the generations to come. And this was the night our baby was conceived, a soul leaving the dry sky of the ancestors to live anew in bones and flesh.

27

I am getting closer to you.

I am exhausted. The pain of this telling is so great that I forget to breathe. I long for your tenderness. For thirty years I have clung to words that might lend me a measure of comfort.

I have longer to please the dead than to please the living. This from Sophocles. Love always protects, always trusts, always hopes, always perseveres. This from St. Paul. What we think we become. This from the Buddha.

28

We were sitting in the Foreign Correspondents' Club at the bar looking over the street and Will came up behind me.

He said, Anne Greves, where have you been? You found him?

I laughed and said, Meet Will Maracle. From Montreal.

Will studied you, said, I remember you. I saw you in a band in Montreal.

You said, That was a long time ago.

Will shrugged, said, I've just come from Siem Riep. There's a scene there. Have you ever been ecstatic in a temple? Know what I think? People have a top brain and a bottom brain. The bottom brain is for survival and seduction. I like the bottom brain. Anyone want a drink?

It felt like home. Meeting old friends. Picking up threads. Jokes. Talk. What life could be like.

Will said, Temple art, bodies falling into hell, shafts of light over the churning sea of milk. Worshiping Shiva in the king. The old guys were very tuned into bottom brain life. Have you seen the carvings? If you could meet any artist, who would you like to meet?

You said, Alive or dead?

Either.

Charlie Mingus.

Will looked at me.

Buddy Guy, no, Will Kemp.

Who? Never mind. I'd like to meet a temple carver. I'd like to know what he thought about when he worked, what he thought when he carved an elephant tossing someone into the air, or Kama dying in his lover's arms. Maybe he was just a laborer with a special skill like me. Maybe he got up in the morning and chipped away all day until he was bone-tired and didn't think about much except where his palm wine was coming from. I want to know how it felt to carve all those apsara breasts. I want to know if he zoned like I do when I work. Time disappears. Those carvers couldn't make a mistake. Imagine a wall carved with a Vishnu lit by solstice light, or a tower of hundreds of apsaras and you're chipping away and you had a bad night and you're not too steady and you chip the wrong way and wreck one of the apsara's Mona Lisa smiles. You'd be fucked.

We laughed.

Acres of carvings, he said, no mistakes, every carving different. Each breast a little different. The carvers must have thought about this. When I stare at the stone faces of the kings I feel their eyes moving, feel them breathing. They look in four directions, waiting until darkness to grab one of those temple dancers, waiting till morning to lose their temper and condemn some poor sod peasant to death. Those haughty eyes, halfway to god, held down by stone necks. I like the bottom brain side of things.

I said, You must have been a carver in another life.

Will said, I only believe in this life. And lots of times I have trouble believing in that.

Will always made me laugh.

You said, We never know which life we are in.

29

Abroad, everyone was talking democracy in Cambodia. They did not talk about fighting and hidden jungle camps, smuggling arms and people, or a minefield called the K5 that stretched from the Gulf of Thailand to the Lao border.

People said, The United Nations will supervise the first elections. Said, Aid organizations must help rebuild. Said, The people are tired of war. Said, The leaders have agreed in Paris to a peaceful transition.

The jungles are so far away from the Champs-Élysée. Each leader hid his own troops: Funcinpec, Son Sann, the Khmer Rouge, the People's Revolutionary Armed Forces. People were refugees inside their own country, starving, killed by bullets, tossed up like little matchsticks along the K5.

You lay on the bed reading a newspaper and I sat at your table studying Khmer. I traced my finger under the curling script and read: *If the tiger lies down, don't say, The tiger is showing respect. If you suspect your wife of being unfaithful, don't let her walk behind you.* I asked, Why are there so many chbaps about suspicion? And you laughed, Because no one can trust anyone.

I picked up your paper and deciphered the headline about more observers coming in for elections. I said, Maybe I could get some translation work with them. Or the UN. I need to work too.

You said, They are useless.

You swung off the bed, pushing the newspaper to the floor, said, The dog barks and the oxcart plods along.

What does that mean?

It means the foreigners come and bark but everything just keeps going the same way.

But someone has to see.

Anne, you do not understand. They try to go into the villages with their white trucks and blue berets and soldiers stop them with guns. At night people in the countryside are made to swallow bullets and the soldiers tell them, If you do not vote as we say, these bullets will explode inside you. They force people to swear before the Buddha how they will vote. They beat people to remind them how to vote. They throw grenades into village leaders' houses. The foreigners go to their comfortable hotels and see nothing. Here's another chbap: The mango and the orange are the same, both sour.

I remembered your fear standing in the kitchen on Bleury Street, holding the last telegram from your father.

I thought we were just two plain people loving each other as best we could. I did not know that you were working for the opposition, taking pictures, writing speeches, translating stories for the West. I had not grasped what was in front of my eyes, that anyone against the government could be murdered for anything. Did you think about why you hid things from me? Was it your habit of long solitude? Was it some antique romance of warriors who return to women after war? Was it my foreignness?

I said, It takes centuries to shape the discipline of freedom. It did in the West, and it takes forever to guard it.

You lifted your hand and waved me away.

Your eyes avoided mine. How could you degrade me with your secret life? I felt your distraction when I touched you. I missed how you used to delight in me. I said, Tell me what you do every morning. I want to see where you work.

It is nothing. Just translation.

Who for?

Whoever needs it. Lots of people.

Where?

You answered roughly, Do not keep asking. What I do is what I do. You suffocate me.

I picked up my purse as if to leave. Fuck you, I said.

You said in a soft voice, Oan samlanh, come here. I am only trying to move on. Do not dwell in the past, do not dream of the future, concentrate the mind on the present moment.

You put your arms around me then. Always your body could melt me, and you knew this and you used this against me.

I said, Do you remember how you were when I first met you? Do you remember how you talked about everything?

You said, We did not talk about everything. You were too young.

I am not young now, I said.

And then you pulled me close. Everything I would forgive you to feel the rough calluses of your fingers against my skin. I was an animal. I could pick up my purse but where in the world could I run to? Out of what despair did you keep your secrets? Out of what fear did I let you? Why did I not make you tell?

30

I often visited old Chan after you left in the morning. She sat in the doorway very, very still but for the tiny jerks of her head, her trauma's unique fingerprint. I brought her bags of rice and fresh greens and fish. Her eyes brightened when she saw me.

The boy-soldiers called Chan Grandmother Fertilizer. She did everything to keep the soldiers from executing her family but not one person survived. I sat in the doorway and listened to her. She cooked me pregnancy teas and told me to eat boiled eggs for my baby. On the day I brought her fresh bananas, she let herself talk.

At first the smell of the corpses made me throw up, she said. I had to peel the flesh from the bodies. I had to gather the bones, burn them and make fertilizer from the ashes. I dragged out the bodies and I did not try to take the flesh immediately; the smell was too bad. I did whatever the boy-soldiers wanted. Sometimes at night I made old-fashioned coin treatments on them. Some of them missed their mothers. Whatever they asked I did. All my children and nephews and nieces were killed. My brothers and sisters were killed near a big tree in Po Penh.

Chan knew everyone on your street when you were growing up. She said, I cooked their medicines and shared my food. I used to listen to Serey singing through the windows. Little Sokha was his shadow. He made Sokha do his chores for him and we laughed at how Sokha wanted to please him. His father was ambitious for them.

She said, The morning Serey left for Montreal his mother's eyes were sun and cloud. She did not want him to go so far.

I asked, Did you ever see Sokha when it was over?

Chan shook her head, All my children are gone. She looked across the broken road and said, Under Sihanouk, people used to greet each other, How many children have you? Under Lon Nol, people said, Are you well? Under the Khmer Rouge, How much food do you get in your cooperative? Now we say, How many of your family are still alive?

I took her hand and I thought of how you once admitted to me in bed that you wished Chan had disappeared instead of your parents.

As if she could overhear my thoughts Chan said, There is nothing for me here. Nothing I can do. The old monks used to say, One day there will be war; the demons come and blood will rise to the elephant's stomach.

The tortured stay tortured. After the bodies were cleared, imagine what people had to do. Imagine the stench that clings.

31

Will, I want to know what he does every day. What happened to your hand?

He was lifting a pitcher of iced tea to fill my glass. We sat at a low table under a big fan in the FCC. Will stretched out his swollen fingers and examined the flesh. He said, Got caught in a dog fight.

He set down the pitcher and scooped out two ice cubes with his other hand. He dropped one into my glass and one into his and after thinking for a long time he said, When people keep secrets it is usually because of shame.

I watched the ice melt.

He said, Imagine what it feels like to come from a place where the tourist attractions are cases of skulls. This guy said to me up at Angkor Wat, Would you want your mother's skull displayed for some stranger to see? What country displays skulls? What use to bring up the past? It will make people want revenge.

I watched the clear morning light on Will's face and said, But to end impunity is not revenge. It is a call for justice.

Will said, That's foreign talk.

Is it?

Can you tell me how people feel after, when you first come in and start digging?

Will stared at my face but he was not looking at me. My ice cube disappeared into the tea.

Numb, he said.

Then he shifted in his chair, said, No one speaks of the stench and the rotting and the decay after. Flies spin in green swarms, settle in heaps on broken glass and broken walls, crawl through cracks, buzz horribly at dawn. Maggots are thick as men's fingers. Rats are bloated with human flesh. The last moving things at night are a handful of stars and the scatter of vermin. People are numb.

But they have to go on. There are convoys of trucks with foreign writing on the sides: UNICEF, OXFAM, CROIX ROUGE. They hauled in rice from Kompong Som and Vietnamese soldiers squatted on the roadsides smoking. There are rumors. People said, Pol Pot arrested his own father for eating a piece of sugar palm and forced him to work in a minefield and he was blown up. People said, He might be coming back. He is still alive gathering a new army on the Thai border. The bridges were gone. The roads were bombed. Everywhere people were starving and trying to walk home. The idea was just to get home. Two million people died. Imagine walking down your street at home and every seventh neighbor dead.

He looked at me, said, Imagine the first real laughter again. Imagine the first time the eyes smile again.

We watched two Australians come through the door with backpacks, drop them on the floor beside the bar and order two beers. I said, I don't understand why you are counting now.

Will said, At first no one really knew what they were doing. Body counters opened a massacre site, measured its perimeter and depth, calculated how many average sized bodies would fit and made their guesses. They did not know about swelling and collapsing and escaping gases. How long the bodies had been there was a crude guess. There were so many massacre sites, Kampong Speu, Prey Veng, Kampong Cham. Now there are better counts: three hundred and nine mass graves, seven sites with thirty to seventy thousand bodies each, twenty-seven sites with ten thousand bodies or more, one hundred and twenty-five sites with a thousand bodies or more. They are in temples and school yards and the jungle. I ask myself, What is the meaning of these numbers?

He studied my face.

I did not know. I imagined the school yard near my father's house. I tried to imagine a thousand bodies there, or seventy thousand. I tried to imagine being left for dead in a mass grave under my father's body, or Berthe's.

Will straightened, said, By the time I got here the graves were disturbed. Pigs, dogs, wild animals, looting, flooding. Peasants went looking for the gold they thought city people took to their graves. People scattered the bones. Or collected them and put them in stupas, or covered them up again. It is hard to get good information. My team went to Laa village and there was this peasant woman who was good at healing. She said she never saw any killing. But one day during Pol Pot time she snuck back to check on her house and her well was full of dead bodies. She covered it with dirt and when the killing was over she moved home and planted a coconut tree on the well but it fell over because the earth was heaving. Too many bodies below. She kept filling the well with dirt and garbage until finally the gases were gone and the worms had done their work and the earth settled. Then she planted a papaya. She said she had bad dreams if she forgot to honor the dead. Her husband said that she had been rewarded for her devotion because she had twice dreamed the numbers of winning lottery tickets. I asked if our team could count the bodies in the well, but she said, Let me think this over.

Old secrets get people in trouble. She did not tell us that her husband had already been down there looking for gold and he only got a few gold teeth. The translator told us the husband said there were twenty-seven skulls in there. When we came back the next morning the old woman burned sticks of incense on the well and she told us that the victims had appeared in her dreams and approved the digging.

She said, Please give me money to hire monks to say prayers over the well.

Our team leader said, We will pay the monks ourselves.

Then Will leaned back, Fuck. They had to fill up the wells and plant again or they would starve. Everything eats everything else. In Kampong Cham people eat intestines and frogs and spiders and fish paste as they have for generations. Here the foreigners go to the Deauville restaurant and eat pâté de foie gras as they have for generations.

He smiled and raised his hands, No one thinks about how all this food is at the top of a food chain fertilized with human flesh. But we gotta eat.

I tossed a balled-up napkin at him and said, I still want to know what Serey is doing when he says he's going to work. And he has never told me what happened to his family.

Will sat forward, crossed his arms on the table, said softly, To know him you need to understand this place.

32

The torturers of Tuol Sleng complained of working long hours, of fatigue. They confessed that it was difficult to prevent themselves from killing in a temper. But they did not complain of the violence. They said, If we did not kill, we would be killed.

You did not want to come with me to Tuol Sleng, Street 103, the hill of the poison tree.

I said, If you do not come I am going anyway. But I want you to come with me.

You said, No use.

Borng samlanh, come. I want to know what you know.

I put my arms around you and you let me and you said, You smell so good.

Tuol Sleng is raw.

It is easy to imagine this place transformed from museum back to extermination center in an hour. Everything left as it was. Burned walls. Bloodstained floors. Metal bed frames and shackles and electrical wires. A barrel of water to submerge a head. People walk over the courtyard graves before they know what they are walking on. There are hand-drawn signs, concrete block rooms, walls of photographs and glass cases of skulls. Paintings of the tortures, fingernails pulled out, men lying in rows on the classroom floors, shackled at the ankles, prisoners beaten and left in tiny cells. The eyes of those whose names disappeared stare from the walls. Their spirits are unprayed for because any family that might have prayed for them is dead. Five thousand photographs of the dead of Tuol Sleng. Each picture refuses anonymity. Boy number 17. He has no shirt and they have safety-pinned his number into his skin. A small woman with the number 17-5-78 pinned on her black shirt stares into the camera and at the bottom of the photo a child's small hand clings to her right sleeve.

Grief changes shape but it does not end.

It was a hot day and your forehead was damp. You said, When I first got back I came here to see if I could find pictures of anyone I knew. Tien's whole family disappeared. I never found anyone who knows what happened to them. In the first months people wrote the names of those they recognized on the pictures. I found no picture to write on.

In Tuol Sleng a person is asked to stare. A person is asked to imagine clubbing someone to death, imagine attaching wires to genitalia, pulling a baby by the ankles away from its screaming mother and smashing its head against a tree.

I was numbed by this vision of a human being. I stood beside you and you were so far away that I could not touch you. In Tuol Sleng a person can be torturer or tortured, a person can imagine a Pure system.

The Khmer Rouge said, Better to kill the innocent than to leave one traitor alive. This is the heart of Purity.

When I was writing this, I dreamed an old woman came to me and said, Help me to see into the darkness. In the dream I protested, How?

See the child.

She has a strong jaw, but her eyes are a child's eyes. Look into the pupils of her eyes. This is a body made vulnerable. This girl is available to wound. She does not even wear a number. She was not even worth a number. This is war. This is the darkness. This child too was murdered in Tuol Sleng.

33

Only seven prisoners came out alive.

We sat in the sun in the courtyard to rest, trying to feel this day again. I touched your hand and you let me.

It was such a pretty day. Bicycle peddlers sold nuts and ice cream outside the walls. Bells rang for a Buddhist wedding. Two taxi drivers were play-wrestling by the gates; the others stood around them, joking and laughing. One lifted the other upside down and he split his pants wide open. They all turned to see if anyone was watching and when I covered my smile with my hand, they ran away. We listened to them collapsing with laughter behind the walls.

Vann Nath was one of the seven who survived. He was selected to paint pictures and shape busts of Pol Pot. If a bust broke and he had to start again, he buried the pieces of the broken one carefully, to show no disrespect. When he painted Pol Pot's skin, he dabbed the brush delicately, to show no disrespect. After it was over he began to paint the tortures, the pictures of Tuol Sleng.

I think of Tuol Sleng and I hear Bach's passion and I hear the thumping rhythms of *Todesfuge* and the chanting of a horrified chorus in *Antigone*. I hear a voice cry out in anguish, If this is a man? Human cruelty turned into a note of music, the rhythm of a sentence. Men have invented a word for this. They call it sublime.

Do not hate me for saying such a thing, borng samlanh. Do not think me perverse. I watched your frantic eyes under your eyelids when you slept, watched the rage and resignation at war under your skin. Borng samlanh, let me look in your place for a while. Do not hate me for naming the Sublime at Tuol Sleng. Do not hate me for wanting to chisel your name, Serey, into the rhythm of my words.

Beside you on the bench in the sunshine that day at Tuol Sleng I said, We must speak what we feel, not what we ought to say.

You said, I feel nothing.

34

Our baby was growing and I found fabric at the Russian market and a teapot, blue colored plates and new chopsticks and a basket for a bassinet.

In the mornings you brought me coffee from the Vietnamese bakery and you ate rice porridge with me but we no longer made love one more time before you left. I loved your dark eyes in the morning.

People live omissions their whole lives. And silence turns into lies.

Here, now, listen to my whisper of shame. As our baby grew, I grew tired of your nightmares. I wish now I had admitted this to you, borng samlanh. I wandered through your city, practicing your language, talking with Sopheap and Chan and Mau, dreaming of teaching again, dreaming of a future. One day I put Chan's hand on my stomach to feel our baby kicking. She grew very still, listening with her experienced old fingers.

She said, A woman needs another woman to lean on so she can find her strength. I will make you a new tea. Your time is getting closer.

Chan's hands had hauled dead bodies. Stripped their flesh. But I wanted their comfort. Dust is dust is dust. Bones work their way to the earth's surface each rainy season. I wanted to feed on joy like the radiant gods.

Against your closed doors I did not want to admit that your pain and silence would be part of our child. I tried to pretend we could make something new. The morning of Pchum Ben I said, Let's go to the temple and make an offering for my mother, for your mother and father and brother. In the shuttered coolness I placed your hand on my stomach and for the first time you felt our baby moving inside me. I watched your wonder and your hair was loose and your eyes were bright. You were so beautiful. When the baby stopped kicking you lay back and said, Samlanh, I will go to the temple with you to make the offerings for our parents but we cannot make an offering for my brother. He survived.

35

You found him by your old front door. You were not sure.

Sokha, is it you? Are you still alive?

You were a stranger to him.

Sokha, it is me, your brother. Sokha, Mak? Pa?

When you said Mak he recognized you. Still he could not speak and you already had your arms around him and you whispered, Our grandmother? Our grandparents in Sras Srang?

You felt his thin fingers on your back and his head shaking no against your neck. You said, I have never felt another body like this on mine. He was bones and skin, but his heart was beating like a rock against mine. And I never wanted to let him go.

Sokha walked from Battambang, passed piles of bodies along the way. He listened to the incessant buzzing of flies crawling over bodies grotesquely swollen. He no longer saw the blue sky or the struggling blossom, only mats of maggots heaving over human flesh. Each time he saw a new pile of bodies he ran away, but the rotting stench of the dead stained the insides of his nostrils. He startled at smells.

All over Cambodia people startle at cigarette smoke and rotting garbage and gasoline, surrogate odors of torture and dead bodies and bombs. A bad smell makes them jump, as people in other places startle at sudden noises. They call this rumseew, making the brain spin. People suffer stiffness in their necks from jerking in the direction of smells. They suffer from dizziness and nausea and call their discomfort a weak heart.

You said, My brother could not bear the smell of meat cooking.

But the city was trying to pick itself up again. Near the palace and the river, food vendors began to push broken carts along the sidewalks and cyclopousse drivers wired old bikes together. People discovered again the passion of speech. They began to shed the disguises they had used to survive. There were those who could not reveal themselves, the torturers, the prison guards, the soldiers. For them there was no exhilaration in language. Virtue is terror, terror virtue. Without slogans, they found themselves speechless.

36

In the yellow bedroom looking over Bleury Street long ago I had listened eagerly to the cheerful stories of your childhood.

Each New Year your family traveled from Phnom Penh up the river to the temples to visit your father's parents in Sras Srang. You flew homemade kites with Leap and the village children along the shore of the lake. You scratched messages into the rocks. Monkeys chitta-chitted from the temples and you said that spirits, neak ta, sramay, were everywhere. There was the story of the outdoor cinema. But I think it was your grandparents who went to it, not you. The traveling cinema came to the village with movies from China and Russia, hung a sheet up near the wat, and families brought their own mats.

Your grandfather fought for Lon Nol and he had an ivory Buddha sewed under the skin on his ankle. He let you and Sokha touch the hard bump through the folds of his old skin. He told you about a short film they always played at the beginning of the cinema. It showed a blindfolded rebel just before sunrise. Twelve Sihanouk soldiers raised their guns and shot at him. One soldier had a blank so no one could know the murderer. Every year this short film played before the movie. The blindfolded rebel died over and over, year after year, his head jerked, the ground splashed with blood, his knees folded beneath him.

You sat up naked in bed to tell this part. You lifted your arms as if you were firing a gun. You put your arms behind your back as if you were the rebel. You fell over dead and I jumped on you and brought you back to life again. Before me, your brother played this game.

You were always first. First to fly a kite, go to school, play an instrument, go abroad. Sokha studied hard in school and your mother praised him. But your father said to him, Are you first like your brother?

Your life and Sokha's was a single stream that divided around a rock, one part falling into thin air over a precipice and the other meandering along the earth in a different direction.

As war came closer, your mother begged to send Sokha to Montreal but your father said, No! How can Serey keep studying and take care of his younger brother?

Sokha said to you, I pretended I could not read. Our leaders said, Reading and writing are unnecessary for the proper cultivation of the earth. Angka is correct, bright and wonderful. I was put in a kang chhlop band to spy. We hid under the floors of stilt houses and listened and reported. I was glad I had no parents to report on. Angka said, Your brigade is the hope of the nation. We repeated, We are the hope of the nation. We sang: *We the children have the good fortune to live the rest of our time in precious harmony under the affectionate care of the Kampuchean revolution, immense, most clear and shining.*

Their words were burned into him. Sokha repeated phrases

you had never heard: Live or die for the greatness of the revolution. Expel all enemies.

Who were enemies?

Those who spoke a foreign language. Those who played music. Those who read and studied. City people. Monks.

Sokha told you he took a message from his unit into the wat behind his camp. In the yard a woman was tied, naked from the waist up, just out of reach of her baby who cried for her breast. The child was not strong enough to sit up, and she could not bend close enough to let him suckle. The woman whispered to Sokha, Help my baby.

A soldier shouted, Move on! Do not worry about her. She will soon be summoned to the mountain.

The revolutionary initiative is self mastery.

There was no radio, no news from outside the forest. The soldiers' way was the only way.

You said to me, While these things were happening to Sokha, I was playing in a band and making love with a sixteen-year-old girl.

Angka never makes a mistake.

It had been a long time since Sokha slept in a room with a door and a roof. You gave him a toothbrush and he had to learn again how to use it. He had to learn again to smile, with his lips, with his eyes. He was tempted by forgotten smells, clean rain, clean skin. But inside his nostrils the air stank of corpses and burning hair and diarrhea. Iron in his soul.

Better to kill an innocent person than to leave an enemy alive.

37

I see your long silence as I see war, an urge to conquer. You used silence to guard your territory and told yourself you were protecting me. I was outside the wall, an intoxicating foreign land to occupy. I wondered what other secrets you guarded. Our disappeared were everywhere, irresistible, in waking, in sleeping, a reason for violence, a reason for forgiveness, destroying the peace we tried to possess, creeping between us as we dreamed, leaving us haunted by the knowledge that history is not redeemed by either peace or war but only fingered to shreds and left to our children. But I could not leave you, and I could not forget, and I did not know what to do, and always I loved you beyond love.

38

The first day of the evacuation of Phnom Penh your family moved only a half kilometer from home, the crowds were so big. Sokha could still see your front door when night fell and he begged your father to let him run back to sleep in his bed. Your father covered his mouth. He said, We will go to Sras Srang and you will sleep in your grandparents' house. Sokha slept in the backseat of the car beside your grandmother. At dawn the soldiers demanded the car and everyone got out except your grandmother. A soldier yelled at your father to give him the keys and he said, Bawng, let us keep it to push my wife's mother in. She is old.

The soldier looked in, said, She is Vietnamese, and he shot her. Your mother screamed and reached for her and the soldier shot her too. Your father grabbed Sokha and whispered, Do not stand up even if they call you, and he threw him into a ditch of tall grasses. The soldiers yelled at your father, Where is the boy? and your father pointed to the opposite side of the road. Then the soldiers shot your father and ran in the direction he pointed. Sokha lay all day in the grass and listened to the sound of people's feet shuffling along the road and soldiers shouting and at night he crawled out of the ditch. He was ten years old. The whole city was walking away and for a while he walked behind another family pretending he was with them.

After you told me this story, you looked out the window and said, All those years in Montreal after they closed the borders, I dreamed of my parents. But they died on the first day. All those years I was dreaming about the dead.

39

I slept the deep sleep of pregnancy. You traced your hand over my skin and you put your ear against my stomach. You said in your soft voice, Is it moving?

This moment is today, or tomorrow. Now that the baby moved, I wanted to call Papa, tell him there would soon be a grandchild, hear his voice, ask forgiveness, offer forgiveness. But I delayed, thinking, Tomorrow, I will call him tomorrow.

I dreamed I was trying to feed a garter snake to a baby. I asked you to kill the snake and you thrashed at it with a stick but when the baby picked it up to eat again it was still alive.

I wakened and watched the early light that bore the city's million songs and the hungry cries of children who did not yet know the stories of this place. I wanted everything for my baby. Your father wanted everything for you. My father wanted everything for me, except the one I loved.

40

The children were taken from their parents to live in children's units. Their leaders sent them to bed, said, Sleep like death.

Sometimes children forgot to put a tool away or stole food. They confessed at rien sot circles each night.

The leaders said, Young comrades, now we will reflect on the day and correct our faults. In this way we cleanse ourselves of mistakes that hinder the revolution.

One boy confessed that he fell asleep after lunch and did not replace the rattan rod on the shelter because of his laziness.

The leader frowned at him, but it was not dangerous because the boy was still a strong worker. Then the leader pointed to the next boy in the circle and that boy said, I did not clean up the supplies shelter today. The leader said, Obey Angka. Angka selects only those who are never tired.

Sokha said, One time I had nothing to report. I had worked hard all day. I had eaten only a half can of rice. I had to think of something so I pointed across the circle at one of the weakest boys and I said, I heard Heng singing an anti-revolutionary song.

The leader's eyes turned hard but he said nothing and sent the boys to bed.

A few nights later Heng was pulled out of his hut. The next day at dawn the children were planting rice and two soldiers came by and threw a boy's body parts into the paddy where they worked.

Fertilizer, they said.

Sokha leaned back and closed his eyes. His dry lips opened and he sang in his still sweet voice:

We the children love Angka limitlessly
The light of revolution, equality and freedom
shines gloriously.
Oh, Angka, we deeply love you.
We resolve to follow your red way.

41

The kites were red and green and golden flying over the river, honoring the wind spirit, Preah Peay, priming the winds to bring the monsoons. In ancient times the kites were called mother-baby kites but now they were called khleng ek because they had a pipe that caught the wind and moaned and whistled, spinning in arcs and twists. The bodies of the kites were great ovals attached to smaller kites shaped like the roof of a temple, and children ran on thin, hard legs while older men trained out the kite strings with patient hands.

We walked from the kite crowds to Wat Phnom where you had fed the monkeys with your grandmother, through food stalls and an open market selling pirated cassette music and videos and carvings and cloth, past the elephant ride at the bottom of the hill and up the steps to the first terrace of the temple. A pair of young orange-robed monks stood on the steps smoking. We set down our bag with water and bread and chocolate and leaned on the wall to rest. A group of students offering prayers for their exams laughed and called to us, Your bag! Your bag! Two monkeys were stealing our picnic. You jumped sideways and clapped your hands and shooed the bold animals back into the shadows of the woods. A man with stumps for legs and one arm and a child also missing an arm appeared noiselessly at my feet. I looked down surprised and handed them some riel from my pocket, asked them their names but they only smiled and said, Security police, as they darted back into the shadows.

On the last small terrace before the temple sat a bird-woman with her bamboo cages of small buntings and swallows and an unfortunate weaver bird. She said in English, You buy? We walked past, but a child with teasing eyes sang out, You no buy, I cry. You no buy, I cry. So I squatted near the little girl and said in English, What are the birds for? She smiled and she was beautiful and in a year or two she would not be safe anymore. She said, For prayers.

I gave her some riel, said, Help me choose one, but the little girl would not so I pointed to a large bunting in front. Her grandmother released the bird and we watched it hesitate before flying up over the top of the temple and away into the trees. I had no wish or prayer. The child would eat that night. The prayer bird would return to the old woman. You held my hand. Our baby turned inside.

If we had looked around we might have seen the footprint of the Buddha on the shadowed paths.

Walking home after dark, you stopped to listen to an eerie wail coming out of the sky and you pointed up, said, Listen. It sounds like the blues.

Above us and over the river flew a small cluster of lantern kites, haunting lights flickering, eks moaning and singing in the darkness. I sensed a thing for which I had no word. Now, still faltering, I might call it prayer.

42

Sokha ran away. He was found by two soldiers in the jungle and he told them he wanted to be a soldier. They laughed and dragged him back to a camp in a small clearing with a few rough sleeping platforms, a cooking fire and provisions shelter. The unit leader looked the boy over and told the soldiers to tie him up. His foot was too small for their leg shackles so they tied a rope around his neck. They left him in the hot sun all day, and at nightfall two new soldiers, one carrying a small ax, the other carrying nothing, untied him and led him into thicker jungle. Sokha thought they were going to kill him when they came to a small clearing in which a man knelt, hands tied behind his back, staked to the ground. As soon as he saw the soldiers he began to beg, Don't kill me, don't kill me. Without a word one of the soldiers lifted the small ax and buried its sharp edge into the man's chest. The man groaned and sank sideways to the ground. The two soldiers looked at Sokha and laughed. They stank of rice whiskey.

Sokha was only trying to survive, you said. Your eyes were dark and dry.

They opened up the man's chest and the older man plunged his hands in, said, One man's liver is another's food.

They placed it on an old stump, and squatted to build a small fire. They drank more and then, poking the liver with a bamboo stick, they sliced and fried it. The blood from the corpse smelled so strong that Sokha threw up and he was afraid that they would kill him for this but they said they were testing his loyalty to Angka and ate the liver and gave some to him to eat too. After that he was taken to be a soldier.

Shame seared me from your burning eyes. I caressed my rounding stomach and tried to protect our baby.

43

Three years. Eight months. Twenty-one days. The Vietnamese invaded and Pol Pot fled north to a jungle camp on the Thai border. Famine. People walking. People trying to find anyone left alive. People trying to go home.

Some soldiers fled to the jungle, to Pailin and the borders. Some leaders began to rebuild to continue skirmishing for another twenty years, trading carvings from the temples, gems and lumber for arms, eating food stolen from refugees. Some soldiers buried their uniforms and returned to their villages. Some hid with missionaries, became Christians. Some tried to hide among half the country's survivors in border camps. Leaders threatened a return to the chaos of Pol Pot and secession of eastern provinces. Jungle camps were alive with young men who knew no way of life but war, restless and waiting.

44

The night Sokha left, you had not seen him for three days. He came in red-eyed and stinking of rice wine.

I am going back to the army in Pailin.

Do not go yet. Not so soon. Stay a little longer.

Sokha held out the wine bottle and after you sipped he swallowed the rest. He said, You did not help us.

The smell of sulfur and rotting wrapped him in a hidden skin. You handed him the photograph of your family and he rubbed the bottom edge with his thumb. You said, Younger brother, what could I do?

Sokha dropped the picture to the floor, said, If I did not obey I would die.

What about the people who did die?

They were secondary victims. If I did not kill, I would be killed. I am like someone who suffered an accident.

Sokha stood without moving and you said, How could you get used to such suffering? Do not go back to them.

Without expression Sokha said, The party called us the heart of the nation. The party said when they arrested someone they never made a mistake.

Even the children? You did not think for yourself at all?

Sokha said, The party told us to repeat, This is the enemy, and I repeated, This is the enemy.

You said, Stay with me. You were just a boy. You do not have to fight anymore.

I have nothing to do here. I like the soldiers.

Live with me. Go to school.

All the teachers are dead. You don't know anything. You were not here.

Then he dropped his bottle on the floor and covered his eyes.

You said to me, He could not recover from what happened. He hated me.

Where is he?

He went north.

We should find him.

Oan samlanh, I have had no word from him for years. I saw him once. He was on the street with government soldiers. He was taller, his face older, like my mother's. I called to him and he looked over and turned away. Can you imagine what it was like? When I first came back, I lost you, and then I found Sokha and lost him too.

Why do you think he hates you?

You looked away and said, I did not see our parents die. I spoke English. I made him do my chores. I was eldest. I never killed anyone. Our father did not send him away too. Maybe he always hated me.

You thought Sokha hated you, but I think you were wrong. The peculiar hatred between brothers is a net warped with doubt and jealousy and buried love. You did not know but Sokha watched you. He knew who you saw, and he gave Will a letter written in red ink warning you to be careful, to go away.

Your name was on their lists.

You were taking pictures of dead bodies and organizing for the opposition, trying to get information out to an indifferent West. I did not know but Will did and the government did.

I was thinking about our baby. I ate what I wanted. I slept when I was tired. My joints were loose. If my body desired, I gave. That pregnancy was so simple. I reached out to you, said, I want you, and you trusted my body too.

I dreamed the smell of warm cotton. I imagined that my mother would have pressed her hand on my stomach to feel my baby. She would have rubbed my skin with scented creams. I imagined what it might have been to ask her to tell me how she felt when I was inside her, to sit with her while I nursed.

Every evening you read the editorials warning people not to oppose the government, threatening violence. People covered things up. Two UN workers who tried to pick up a body on the riverbank were expelled. You threw the newspaper down in disgust.

I asked, Do you think if there was a trial, a truth commission, the country could move on?

You said with irritation, If the leaders have not changed, it is our duty to judge them, not to forgive them. We cannot build on lies and violence. Would you have accepted this in Montreal?

The elections were heating up. We all saw the truckloads of young soldiers riding through Phnom Penh with their AK-47s. We all knew about the bandits on the roads out of town at night, the impoverished soldiers who ran roadblocks and stopped foreigners from getting into the villages. Will knew they were targeting people like you who worked for the opposition. Later, when I accused him of silence, he said with a shrug, I never interfere with lovers.

45

I can still see a particle of dust hanging in a sunbeam near your cheek as you slept.

46

On Christmas Day we drove to the temple in Udong along the road to Tonle Bati. I thought of Christmases with Papa and how we always put my mother's star on the top of the Christmas tree on Christmas Eve and always walked up the mountain and slid on Beaver Lake on Christmas morning and always went to Berthe's for an old-fashioned goose in the late afternoon. Papa always bought pebber nodders, cinnamon and cardamom short-breads and krasekagers for dessert on Christmas night and Berthe served them with her bûche de Noël and tartelettes au sucre. I mailed Papa a letter without a return address wishing him a merry Christmas and telling him about the baby. I thought I might call him that day but I did not. I could not bear to hear his voice.

When your mother was expecting Sokha, your parents took you to Udong. Outside the temple a pinpeat band, each man blinded or missing a limb. Simple rhythms of the samphor played by a young man with open, unseeing eyes, small finger cymbals played by a legless man with angry lines between his eyebrows, two bamboo roneat played by older men who swayed over their long xylophones. The sound of this music natural as wind in the trees. You took coins from your pocket and threw them on a bit of cloth in front of the orchestra. These were lives cut in two, the time before they stepped on the landmine and the time after. We went into the temple and you led me to a carved relief of a husband and wife bowing before a midwife.

Why is she wearing a box on her head?

That box holds the afterbirth, you said. She has to wear it on her head because she did not pay the midwife enough respect.

Thank god I have no midwife, I said.

I know. You are not from here.

Did your mother have a midwife?

No. They were modern. My father wanted her to go to a hospital.

Then if we do not have a midwife, we follow your family tradition.

You put your arm around my waist and spoke in your soft, warm voice, Tradition does not matter now. We can do things our own way because they are all dead.

47

You risked your life, and mine and our baby's, but you did not tell me what you were doing and you could not stop yourself.

And I am past care.

48

I like the comfortable melancholy of pregnancy, waiting, both fierce and vulnerable. I often walked in the market and when Mau was there, I would bring him a sweet drink and sit with him under the yellow fringe of his remorque. One day we watched a young boy trying to sell postcards to a European tourist wearing leather shoes. The boy followed the big man and thrust the cards in front of him. The man took a card and looked at it and handed it back shaking his head. The boy kept following him. Three times the man turned away and finally he reached in his pocket and handed him some crumpled riel to get rid of him. The boy angrily threw it on the ground and said in English, I am not begging. I am selling. I want to go to school.

I glanced at Mau but he pretended he had seen nothing.

Mau, do you have children?

Two sons, borng srei.

How old are they?

The eldest is nine and the younger five. My wife takes them to school every day. We must protect them from being taken.

Taken?

For ransom, he said. But there was pride because he had money.

Why did you come to Phnom Penh?

I am from Kep, and my wife's family is from Ang Tasom. After the war we came here to find work.

His face closed. No more questions.

I shifted to ease my back and watched people eating their noon meals from tin boxes or folded papers. I said, Will you come with your family to see a Yike show tonight?

Mau was pleased, said, Borng srei, I have work to do now. I will come and pick you up later.

He arrived in the early evening, his sons dressed in clean white shirts. His wife, Ary, smiled at me and said, I no English, and nudged her eldest son, Nuon, forward and the boy said in English, I am pleased to meet you, and without being pushed his little brother, Voy, stepped forward and said in English, I am your friend.

Mau said, Maybe you will teach them more English when they are older.

You climbed lightly into the remorque with the boys and pulled a string from your pocket to play your old string game. Ary sat on the opposite bench with me. We drove past the palace and turned down the long shaded avenue through the gates of the Royal University. The walls were pocked with bullet holes. Mau paid a driver he knew to watch his remorque. You led us along a broken pathway, not to a theater but to a large studio where dancers were practicing. We stood at the edge of open doors to watch an old woman coaching a group of young girls in traditional court dances. On powerful thighs young barefoot dancers dipped and rose, training their arms and hands and heads and eyes to centuries-old movements that had almost been lost. The old woman slipped among them, touching a hand to bend it back at the wrist, shaping the fingers, gently correcting, demanding uncompromised perfection. She was small and wore a simple blouse and a plain sampot wrapped around her old woman's waist and she moved with quick, energetic steps, dipping at the knees, arms rippling and hands opening and closing like roses. You said, Em Theay lived in the palace as a child and was a favorite of the queen. She teaches hours every day, trying to save the dances.

Her gray hair was pulled back simply under a cloth headband and when she showed a movement, her heart-shaped face lifted toward the sky, the deep creases in her old face smoothed, arms lifted lightly from dropped shoulders, fingers stretched backward, thumbs in the opposite direction, hands turning on her wrists like petals on a stem.

We left the dancers and walked across the campus to the stage where the Yike performers sat in a half circle already singing together the song of Toeup Sodachan. Ary settled her sons, telling them soon the devada was coming. Together we watched the old play once performed near wats and rice fields, the story of a devada goddess forced to come to earth in human form. She was condemned to serve a slave from whom she had stolen a flower. The devada-girl helped the slave gain his freedom and we watched with caught breath the moment they first expressed their love, the birth of their child, and then we watched with outrage and sorrow when the devada was told that she must leave her earth family because her banishment from heaven was over. You took my hand and stroked it as the grieving couple separated, their child in the husband's arms. The man opened his throat and sang, asking heaven what divine justice would separate a mother from her child. You whispered to me, I once heard Sin Sisamouth sing this part.

Borng samlanh, our baby was rolling inside me as I watched the performer standing alone singing his anguish to the sky, and these memories are threaded through with the eyes of Tuol Sleng, with images of babies torn from their mothers by soldiers, of babies tossed and shot in the air. I wondered what had become of me that I could not stop seeing such things. I looked around the audience and saw people wiping their eyes and little Voy had fallen asleep and Mau picked him up and we walked back to the remorque. Ary followed, holding Nuon's hand in the unlit night. Mau drove us home through the dark streets, past the palace where the bats had already flown out in black clouds for their night feeding. When I said good-bye, he said quietly, Borng srei, my wife will help you when your baby comes.

As we climbed the stairs to our room you said, I have never been back to the theater in all the years. I always used to go with my family.

I said, After the baby, let's find Sokha.

I do not think he wants to be found. He is not like a brother anymore.

I said, Borng samlanh, families forgive and go on and come in all shapes. He is all you have.

But you joked it away with your charming smile, Yes, samlanh, and you are my family now and you are big as an elephant. Maybe there are two in there.

49

The hot dry season was on us and weekends we drove out of the city down the narrowing road to Kien Svay. Food stands selling fresh pomelos and jackfruit. Ice cream sellers held up lotus-shaped treats on bamboo sticks. The vendors laughed and raised their eyebrows and looked at each other when they heard me speak Khmer. A country girl asked, What province are you from?

An old woman yelled at a young man who rode his motor-cycle too close to her stall. Past the sign to Koki we saw woven huts on stilts rising out of the water where city people picnicked in the cool breezes. I did not want to go that day, I felt too warm and a little ill. But you said, Come, the coolness on the river will be good for you. We bought cooked river lobster and fruit and tied them in a cloth. We rented a river hut and hired a boatman to take us out. People sat on rented river platforms eating and playing cards and talking. We tore the shells off the lobster and threw them in the water. You always ate slowly, as if there were too much food. I peeled some fruit with my pocketknife and laid it on a bit of paper. I shifted on the mat and finally lay on my side looking at the sky. I was growing warmer and my body ached and I said, Maybe we should go back.

You looked across the water as if you had not heard, said, When I first met you, I had no burden of family. I dressed and ate and slept how I wanted. I played the music I wanted. I dreamed of going back home. But I no longer followed the way of my ancestors. I was becoming someone new. I thought, By surrendering all that one thinks of as self, self is found. But that changed when I got back here. I cannot stop thinking of what I lost. You caressed the round hardness of my stomach, said, My grandmother told me, Do not pursue the past. Do not lose yourself in the future.

I pressed your hand over our baby moving and said, We do not stop missing the ones we lose.

You looked across the river, said, A person can get used to anything. I love you, Anne.

That night, I knelt face down on the bed, knees spread, and I gave myself to your love. My body was yours. I trusted you. When we lay apart, side by side, I could still feel the print of your hands on my breasts, the thickness of you trying to make yourself reborn between my legs. I dozed and stirred awake and I felt the baby turn inside clear as a word. I was still unwell and beginning to sweat.

You were lying awake and when I took your hand you said, They say that the souls of the dead wander if the monks don't pray over the bodies. But I think the souls of the living wander when their dead are lost.

A deep ache moved through my joints. I squeezed your arm, said, Could you bring me some water? I am burning up.

50

There are terrible fevers and a sick lassitude unique to the tropics, a torpor that sent me into dreams of drowning in crystal waters, clean, cold northern lakes bubbling over my head and I lay on the bottom looking up to the surface but I could not move. I knew that if I did not get up I would drown but in the dreams it did not bother me. The worst pain was behind my eyes and my nose. My gums bled and my knees and shoulders ached and I shivered in the heat as if I were freezing to death. On the third day little islands of rash appeared all over my body and you wrapped me in blankets and held spoonfuls of water to my lips. Finally on the fifth day you said, I must find a doctor. There were so few doctors. You drove me in the sidecar to Calmette Hospital. We passed soldiers riding in open trucks and you turned your face from them. The doctor examined me and frowned. This is dengue, he said, breakbone fever, infection. They put me in a long ward because I was pregnant, and I lost consciousness as if I were in shock, and when I finally woke two days later you were sitting beside me and the doctor was listening with a stethoscope to my stomach. That evening the fevers finally broke and you fed me a clear soup and the doctor returned. He spoke in the neutral tone of one charged with bad news. I wanted to thrash him with a bamboo stick. I wanted to make him tremble and grovel, make him beg for his own life. I wanted to scream no no no, make time turn back. You hung my sweat-soaked sheets to dry. You moistened my lips with a cloth and combed my hair. You put your hand on my stomach and I slowly admitted an unfamiliar stillness inside. How many days had our baby not moved while I lay in the fever? I tried to make myself believe that the doctor was mistaken. I wished if our baby were dead that I might die with it and when the doctor told me they would induce it in the morning, that I would deliver it dead, I pretended it was not happening, that they were wrong. I wanted my baby alive, I wanted you to be far away with me, I wanted, I wanted. You brought me soup and said, I will go find something to eat and come back soon.

Will took you to one of the beer gardens on the east bank of the river. I never went to those places where girls dressed in the colored uniforms of Stella Artois and Becks and Carlsberg, where drunken men sat under strings of colored lights and girls slipped away from the casual pats and squeezes of men's hands saying, Please uncle, try my beer, and bent their ears to men's lips to make special arrangements. You were coming back to me when you heard a gunshot on the side of the road.

People stared as the man crumpled to the ground. A motorbike was slowly pulling away, the man on the back riding pillion, holding a rifle. A hundred meters down the road, the bike turned and doubled back. People began to scatter but Will stayed and knelt by the man in a wreath of blood without looking at the bike. The killers made no effort to hide their faces with sunglasses or helmets. They rode back and slowed and they looked to be sure they had hit their mark. With dread certainty you knew then and you said to Will, The driver.

Will ignored you, said, I think he's still alive.

He cradled the back of the man's head, laid his other hand over the wound, murmured to him. Someone yelled at Will in Khmer, Don't touch him.

You stepped toward Will, said in English, Get away from him.

Will bent lower and slid his palm to the man's face, said without looking away from his eyes, The guy's dying.

You watched the motorbike circle back a third time and now the side of the road was deserted and the voices in the beer garden fell silent. Thai pop music from tinny speakers. Strings of red and blue and green lights over deserted tables. When the motorbike stopped and idled beside the dying man, Will looked up and said over the engine noise, You fucks. The driver yelled, Chohp! and you said to him in Khmer, He does not understand you. Please, Sokha.

Sokha finally saw you and his startled eyes locked with yours. You bent slowly toward Will and said in Khmer to the men on the motorbike, Muy soam, leave the foreigner out of it, he doesn't understand what you say. I'll take him away. Without any sudden movement you reached down to Will's shoulder, grasped his shirt.

Will was already releasing the man's head gently to the road and he stood stiffly and wiped his bloody hands on his pants. He said to no one, He's dead.

The man on the back of the bike still had his gun raised and Sokha shifted into gear, revved and pulled away.

You said, Let's go.

Together you came back to the hospital. You smelled of outside air. I saw the stains on Will's pants, pulled myself up, looked at your pale face. Will said, They're shooting people on the street.

I looked at his dirty fingernails, asked, You saw?

A journalist, you said.

Will sat on the edge of my cot and you smoothed the sheet near my hand, pulled the crumpled blanket flat over my swollen breasts, said, It was my brother driving the gunman.

Sokha?

He was going to fucking kill me, said Will.

The skin around your eyes was taut.

No, he wasn't, you said. They got who they wanted. And you straightened the corners of the bottom sheet into neat, tight folds.

Will shifted and jostled me on the cot, Get him the hell out. His own brother.

I smelled their sweat. I loathed the excitement I felt in their fear. Their squabbling. I thought, I have this dead baby. Why do they come to me with this?

Will took my hand and squeezed it and saw me for the first time. He said, You should be resting. What are we doing?

You had turned your back to us and stood looking down the ward and Will said, We should go.

But you shook your head, I'll stay here tonight.

You handed Will your keys and walked down the ward with him and when you came back you sat beside me on the bed and you took my hand and talked softly for a long time. Spoke of Sokha, his startled eyes that went hard as old coins, said, I was so afraid. Then you told me about the dying man on the street. Your eyes were dark ringed. You whispered in English so no one on the ward would understand, whispered his name, that he had written against the government, said you had worked with him. I watched the shadows across your weary face and you said, I have not told you things, Anne. I should have.

What haven't you told me?

Your hands were cold on mine and you said, I need to think.

Think?

Please, oan samlanh. Tomorrow we can talk, after it is over.

Serey, I said. Why are you doing this? Tonight?

But you only shrugged, and turned from me. Methodically you found a frayed mat, settled on your side on the floor beside my bed and slept the deep sleep of a guilty man when a decision has been made.

51

It was a savage old-fashioned procedure with a metal curette and soon my body was nothing but wave after wave of roiling pain. Deliver this dead fetus. Deliver my first baby. The doctor worked and worked, massaged me, as if he were tearing me apart, and I pushed and he guided my baby's head and I pushed. You tried to hold my hands but my fists were clenched around balls of rough cotton sheet. There was only pain. Me alive, my dead baby out. To this end the doctor used his skills. Your eyes held mine and I saw in their reflection a desperate animal trying to survive. I pushed and pushed again and I was lost in pain and trying to escape drowning in your eyes and after they cut the cord I had to push again to get rid of the afterbirth but this word is wrong because it was after death. They wiped her off and gave her to you to hold. She was a perfect little girl with your mouth, I saw her in your arms, our dead daughter, and you brought her close to me to see and I cupped her cheek with my hand and it was still warm and then with grace beyond measure I saw you hand her to the nurse and turn back to the mess on the delivery bed, blood, shit, amniotic fluid, me.

My milk came in and I wept with the startling prickling pain of my breasts swelling and a nurse showed me how to express the milk into a metal pan. Gently she asked, Could I use it for another baby? There is need. Crying, I nodded, thought, how long will I feed another baby? How does the milk stop? My tears hardened molten. When I think now about that time I am astonished at how my body regathered, moved on, left my soul behind.

They bound my breasts and got me up because they needed my bed. You signed papers and we were allowed to take our dead daughter to be cremated at the temple near the Globe and in the sidecar I held that cold small body wrapped in a square of white cotton and we paid four monks for prayers and as I stood with them thinking about my baby, my bindings and blouse became soaked with milk and when the ceremonies were over you said, Let's go home.

I said, Which home?

My aching breasts. The hot wind in the sidecar. You stopped by the shrine under the tree near Independence Monument, put some fruit there and said without looking at me, I have been working for the opposition, samlanh. I am sorry you found out this way. I wanted to tell you.

When our eyes met I saw in yours a light that did not seek me. You had a driven look I recognized, a look that still desires to be loved, that tolerates no obstacle, that bargains. You said, This is a disheveled country. I want to go away with you but I cannot bring myself to leave. What have I done?

I pushed your hand away and said, You know what you are doing. Do not pretend you are sorry.

We will try again. I will be all right. Don't worry.

I did not want to leave without you. I did not want to stay. You wrapped your arms around me and I let you, and you whisper-sang and I was melting all over again, listening to the voice I loved in front of a shrine I did not believe in, our Eros tangled into loss and grief. And I wondered who you were and we were fallen, fallen.

52

Mau came to our room with Ary. She wore a plain wrapped skirt and white cotton blouse and she entered without making a sound on the floor, not looking at anything but me. Mau hung back in the door frame and I pulled myself up in bed. I asked, How are Nuon, Voy?

Ary was already at my bedside and gently she said, Very naughty. We brought you special tea, very good for you.

Mau gave her sharp directions in a muttered, rapid Khmer I could not understand. She poured the tea from a thermos and placed it on a small table beside the bed and then Mau spoke and she picked it up and held it to my lips. Her hands were cool. I took the cup and held it myself and she swept the room and straightened the sheets. She kept her back to her husband and sat on the edge of the bed and smoothed my hair and wiped my face with a cool cloth and took my hands in hers. Her eyes held mine and she said softly in Khmer, Soon you will feel better. You crossed the river too soon but you will try again. A woman is strong.

Her eyes held my grief, and her body gathered in my pain and knit it into herself as if she were an old marsh creature weaving baskets from rushes.

Our dead daughter's tiny face. Your mouth. Your eyes. I have lost some of memory's shards but not this one.

53

The Phnom Penh where you disappeared was corrupt as hell. Anyone could buy a pillowcase of dope for twenty dollars, or a girl or a boy for the price of a meal. Judges made judgments after they received an envelope. Police gave tickets after the bribe.

Easter, March 31. Elections coming. Truckloads of armed soldiers roared through the streets. Foreigners retreated into their apartments and to the airports. Some leaders were talking this thing, democracy, and expatriates with their pasty skin and their money and their partial understandings were again chirping unfamiliar words, free-and-fair, in different languages. They talked about observing elections but no one saw the village meetings after dark when people were told how to vote and people who asked questions were beaten, killed. Foreigners said, Keep the eyes of the world here, but the people knew that borders and banks close and foreigners leave and wires are cut and bodies disappear and the thirst for power spreads like the odor of rotting, terrifying everyone into obedience. A man with a gun can force a child to kill. No one can force compassion. But it can be extinguished.

Easter Sunday. A speech at the National Assembly.

Ordinary people came to hear the opposition. People showed peculiar courage, by gathering, by listening, seduced by the possibility of a different life. They walked in front of guns. They stood out in the open. Prime Minister Hun Sen, peering from his one good eye, was irked. It was time to shave a few strokes off the golf score.

You should have known. I loved your eyes in the mornings. When you left me that morning you said, See you later. Why were you there? The place was surrounded by B40 rocket launchers. It backed onto Hun Sen's house.

Sopheap pushed her noodle stand to the edge of the gathering. Her baby slept in a sling on her back and she held her toddler's hand. People in crowds were always hungry after speeches. She could make good money here. Sam Rainsy stood on a wooden chair and talked about the future. He wore a suit and a yellow tie and a man behind his chair started applause after each important phrase. The bodyguard stood at his right shoulder and his followers clustered in front of him waving light and dark blue flags.

Oppose corruption, said Sam Rainsy. Stop bribes. Stop beatings. Create a better country for your children.

Sopheap gave her little girl a piece of sugarcane to chew so she could listen to the leader. Peaceful. Then: pop. The center of the crowd fell flat to the ground but those who did not recognize the sound of the pin pulled from a grenade did not drop fast enough. Their bodies took the ragged metal disks. Shrapnel cut off feet, sliced through calves, cracked knees.

Before the second grenade, a bodyguard knocked Sam Rainsy off his chair and covered him up and died from the explosion. Pop. People crumpled like marionettes with cut strings.

Pop. Factory workers on the west side of the crowd got it.

Pop. Sopheap and her baby and her toddler chewing sugar-cane and the other street vendors with their noodles and cigarettes and buns at the back of the crowd were tossed up into the air beside their splintering carts. Sopheap's baby was blown out of her hands and her toddler was flung backward and shrapnel sliced into Sopheap's chest. Her noodle stand exploded into handfuls of toothpicks and everything fell in slow motion back to the earth.

The injured lay with the dead, and after the first shocked silence, low moaning. Then tiny movements, an arm, a finger. Voices pled for help and soldiers with guns ordered the weeping onlookers not to touch anyone. The police roped off the area and pulled down the loudspeakers. The dying groaned, Please, please.

A few ambulances came after a long, long time.

The hospital floors were slippery with blood. Workers hosed down halls. People lay on worn mats. I listened to their whispers. We were only listening to a speech, they said. Their bodies were pitted with other people's skin. Their faces cut. I did not find you. I found Sopheap. Dead. I did not find her baby or her little girl. On the second day in the early morning, I went again. Nothing. On the third day the floors were scrubbed clean and everyone who was at the Easter rally was either dead or silent. I wanted to rub ashes on my face. I saw a young man who looked like you on the street but he was wearing army clothes and carried an AK-47 under his arm. I did not know where to look. I went everywhere: police stations and political offices and the United Nations and embassies and consulates and army offices. Someone knew. Someone had to tell. I dreamed of blood and boars in forests.

I have money. Where is he?

I fell in love with you, and my whole self became yours— without my wanting or not wanting it. I loved being alone in the dark with you, walking on dark streets heading always to some kind of makeshift bed behind a door that closes. Always we met at the end of the day. Since the first time I made love with you I have never once come to the end of the day and not waited for you to be there. Waiting for me. Standing at my door. On the street. Inside my room. At the station. This feeling all through the days that we were together and the years that we have been apart. Each day I imagined you because if I did not, joy would vanish. You cannot disappear. Please do not disappear. No one can mend my sorrow. I love what I lost.

I went to look for you at the city wats where they dumped bodies. I saw other bodies. Never yours. Will walked with me on the riverbank, down below the palace where other bodies showed up. We found a young man, in his twenties, jeans stolen, shot through the chest. There was bloating and Will said, Don't look, you don't need to see this.

Why don't I need to see, Will? I see dead bodies on the front pages of newspapers every day. Television is full of dead bodies. But I am not supposed to look at one man lying in front of me, left because the ones who love him are afraid to claim him, because they do not know where he is. Because the government leaves bodies like little notes written in red. Tell me, Will, why should I not look?

Will said, All right. I just thought.

We left the riverbank and went to report the body at the police station. The officer said, He must have suffered an accident.

I said, I am looking for someone else who disappeared from the rally.

He gazed at me and said, This is not possible.

To live I was condemned to hope.

I leaned in close to his ear, said, *I have money*. He was at the grenade attack at the palace. What happened to him?

There was no sign of you at all from the churning sea of blood.

54

Everyone had interests. To keep the lid on violence. To keep power. To get power. No point to stir up the past, they said. What if leaders want to take revenge? If leaders do not get a correct result from this voting, we will return to Pol Pot times. They said this. People in the opposition began to hide or flee. All nineteen of the opposition newspapers closed. This strange new food called democracy did not taste as the people imagined. How to make democracy from centuries of kings, occupation, war, genocide? Why is this new fresh rice filled with pebbles?

I was on the other side of history. Do not let an angry man wash dishes; do not let a hungry man guard rice.

My only worth was my desire. To find you.

Men called me foolish, stubborn, worthless, naive, foreign, selfish, stupid, a woman. I wanted what I wanted; I claimed my own lucidity.

I have money. What happened to him?

I have remained silent in the chasm between knowledge and silence, between the law and love. It was so easy for the state to silence me, to say, You have no right. Thirty years and I still want to scream in disbelief. No right?

I have money. Where is he?

I slept with the lights on. I slept for an hour and woke and was sleepless again. I lived in the exhaustion of grief.

Rotting fruit at a shrine under a tree. The glint of sunlight on the river. A child holding a baby on her hip in a doorway. I walked and did not know where I had been or how long I had been gone.

I have money. Where is he?

55

On Bonn Pchum Ben, a day to honor the ancestors, people dress in clean clothes and go to the temples to bring food to the dead. The souls of the dead return each year for food and my little daughter had never tasted food at all. I bought the best bay ben, rice balls filled with coconut and beans and sesame seeds, so that her first taste of food would be delicious, and I went to the temple where she was cremated and slipped off my shoes at the door. I burned a stick of sandalwood incense for her and made my food offering to the monks and then I knelt and said prayers for my daughter in the darkened, sweet smelling gloom, under the gaze of an orange-robed Buddha. Hundreds of candles flickered in the darkness. I did not believe and yet I knelt with all the others and watched the smoke of the incense twist toward the roof. I did not want to leave. I had nowhere to go. I wanted comfort. The end of the rains. I did not believe and yet I was there. I closed my eyes and stayed and prayed in English, the words of my childhood, because that god too was a compassionate god, and I prayed for my mother and I prayed to see you again. And when I opened my eyes and lifted my head I noticed a young monk watching me curiously and I thought, What am I going to do?

In bed that night I woke from another restless sleep, my clitoris erect, my labia filled and swollen. It felt like rain. In the desolate darkness my animal nature begged and I thought, So part of me is still alive but I cannot be alive if you are dead. I lay alone and let my body have its way. And then I fell asleep so deeply that when I woke the sun was halfway toward noon and my body was refreshed. I stretched in the thick heat knowing that my grief was changing shape and I did not feel relief or joy but the emptiness of one who lives on.

Will met me at the FCC most nights for something to eat and he said, You better stop asking around. They told me to warn you. Don't draw attention to yourself. I am leaving. I am just waiting for my ticket. Come with me. Things cook up out of mild beginnings.

I ran my fingers through my hair and a clump came out in my hands.

Everyone was trying to bury a bit of rice, to hide a little money. Everyone was buying and selling. The streets grew silent and empty and no one knew if the country was collapsing, if everyone would starve again. People hurried to work with their heads down and hastened through the markets. Soon the river would change direction and in great turbulence turn around and flow north. And the long grasses and reeds on the river-banks hid bodies and there seemed to be no fresh water capable of turning the violence around.

A young soldier slipped into the shadow of a side street beside me and whispered in my ear, I know where he is. Do you have money?

I said, Half now, half after you tell. I unfolded an American twenty inside my pocket, pulled it out and put it on his palm. He eyed the bill and slipped it into his pocket. He said, They took him to Ang Tasom.

Is he alive?

This is all I know. They took him to Ang Tasom.

Are you telling the truth?

He held his open hand out between us again. His eyes were thin black knives and I could not tell if their glint shone with malice or fear.

I said, That is not much. But I handed him the bill he believed he was owed and he disappeared back into the shadows.

Ang Tasom

56

Before dawn I went to find Mau at Psar Tuol Tom Pong. The drivers sitting on their motos and tuk tuks outside the market said, He's not here yet.

I asked them, How long to drive to Ang Tasom?

A young man with a good moto said, The road to Ang Tasom has many holes, very slow, dancing road. My friend can take you in a car.

How long does it take in a car?

A half day, borng srei. Not long. Faster in a car. I will give you a good price.

When Mau arrived I said, I want you to help me find him. I want you to take me to Ang Tasom.

Mau said, This is not good, borng srei. Even if you find him, what can you do?

I said, If I do not find him, how can I live?

Two drivers who were listening stepped forward and Mau stood up. He said, Okay, I will take you. My wife has family there. I cannot promise but I will try. I need money for gas.

He left me at Will's, then went to tell Ary. I ran upstairs to Will's room.

I heard Will get out of bed and when he opened the door he was still slipping one arm through the sleeve of a dirty yellow T-shirt. He said, Anne, people say anything for a dollar. Even if it is true, they want him disappeared.

He was barefoot and his hair was tangled and there were smudges under his eyes.

You look terrible.

Thank you. I just got to bed.

I can see. I am leaving now. Come with me. Come, you can sleep on the way.

What makes you think they'll *let* you find him?

I have already started to find him. They have no right to hide him.

No one has rights here. You are not going to find him. It's not gonna happen.

It already *is* happening.

Anne, two tourists got pulled off a train and shot in Kep this week. People are going missing. The embassies won't help. The banks are closed. I'm not screwing with this government.

Fine. I am not begging. Even if you offered to come, I wouldn't let you.

Will looked out and saw Mau down below. He was beating dust from the yellow fringe, had extra gas in two Fanta bottles under the seat. Will turned to me, said, Why Mau? Why not a four-wheel-drive with some air-con? Why not a car with windows that open and close?

I said, A moto never gets stuck. I trust Mau. He knows people there.

Will shrugged, said, Wait a minute.

He packed a small rucksack, threw in some bottles of water,

found his shoes, tied a krama around his neck. He said, There are things people regret not doing. I don't think this would have been one of them.

When Mau saw Will get in the remorque he smiled and pulled down his Chicago Cubs cap, slipped his bike into gear and cut into the slow motion traffic, past an oxcart piled with wood, past a white Toyota van. The swaying fringe behind Will's head looked like an old-fashioned lampshade.

A prayer bird flew up from a temple. Over the riverbanks were vultures, and circling above the eddying river a falcon. I said to Will, We should make it in less than a day. Maybe by tonight I will know what happened.

Will said, There are many wonders in the world. But none so wonderful as a human being.

Along the quay two street sweepers already worked in the cool of morning, kritsh, kritsh, bent creatures making a few riel a day, their straw brooms herding eternal dust. One stopped to make an offering under a tree. What did she pray for? Who would I pray to? I believe in no god but I burn incense and give food to the dead, to the monks, repeat old prayers. It is not necessary to complete the work, but neither are we free to desist from it. I watched some red-collared doves pecking on the pavement and heard a cuckoo-shrike in a tree down the quay.

The Phnom Penh we were leaving was subdued. Former leaders were disappearing across the border, the government demanded uncontested victory, everyone was trying to protect interests, secrets, the world looked away so that things could appear to be free, all solutions delicate, political, violent.

As we rolled through the streets we watched early morning people hasten along. In craving. In need. All over Phnom Penh people were waking and rubbing their eyes, making ready to survive another day. Through a window I watched a woman wipe and swaddle her baby. The older children had to do for themselves.

On the river, rusty pocket freighters, fishermen poling along the shores, a police boat already roaring by.

I watched the waking city and prayed for you to be alive.

Will touched my leg and pointed with his eyes to a young woman walking up a side street, hand resting lightly on the arm of a child. I could not see her face, only her thin, erect back. Will said, There's Sineth. As we drove by I turned to see the woman with the beautiful lips from Seeing Hands, her face without eyes or nose, the flattened patched skin graft scarred tight to her forehead and her lips. She walked gracefully, and Will said, She's going to work. I was supposed to go say good-bye to her today.

Long ago, when they emptied Phnom Penh, closed the borders, people remembered things, the last time they slept in a bed, the last time they saw a loved one. There was that last telegram out of Phnom Penh before all lines to the outside world were cut: I ALONE IN POST OFFICE. LOSING CONTACT WITH OTHERS. I AM TREMBLING. HOW QUIET THE STREETS. NOWHERE TO HIDE. MAY BE LAST CABLE TODAY AND FOREVER.

Calm when the end is near. Calm, from the word for heat.

57

Kathen festival. Outside the city, everywhere people made offerings for merit. Tables in front of the temples, tinny loudspeakers blaring, hands and baskets outstretched for alms. Monks stayed in monasteries through the rainy season and wore their old robes until the people brought them new ones on the last day of Kathen. Dirt and cleansing. Death and rebirth. Wet season and dry. After we crossed the agitated river, temple music mixed into the dust of the road.

What I have left is sand running through the narrow opening of an hourglass, grains falling, and falling again, and falling again, like a stick beating someone to death, and never stopping and never disappearing.

At the first pagoda gate, Mau got off his moto and looked down the path toward the temple. A monk appeared and Mau offered him some worn riel from his thin pocket. I asked the ajah to bless our remorque and our journey. I tied a krama over my nose and mouth against the dust as country women do.

Fifteen kilometers out of Phnom Penh, the first market. Ropes of meat hung from bamboo poles under the thatch roofs of the sausage stalls. Steam rose from pots of boiling water and orange coolers hid bottles of colored sugar water and Coke. Small tables and kitchen chairs were tucked under the shade for hungry travelers.

Twenty-four kilometers farther, the flats and dikes. Mau worked hard to keep us out of the ruts and mud. Soon now, nothing but paddies of green rice shoots stretching to the horizon, bits of scrubby bush and sugar palms, blue shadows of mountains in the west. No one but farmers and their oxen. Will rolled a joint and offered it to me. I stared at the paddies and felt the hot air on my toes. We bumped past skinny, barefoot kids not in school, past people cooking food to sell, wiping the leaves of money plants near their stalls. My mind slowed and spread against the wide fields.

Why do some people live a comfortable life and others live one that is horror-filled? What part of ourselves do we shave off so we can keep on eating while others starve? If women, children, and old people were being murdered a hundred miles from here, would we not run to help? Why do we stop this decision of the heart when the distance is three thousand miles instead of a hundred? I stared as far as the Elephant Mountains. I liked the road, moving, being nowhere.

Will leaned back, eyes half closed.

I said, How do you measure time?

He said without opening his eyes, By how long it takes to get stoned.

At home I used to measure time by when I first heard the song of the white-throated sparrow in spring. How long does it take a body to go cold?

Will frowned, Can you not just relax for even one moment?

I laughed.

I was a warrior, stoned, sleepless, heading for battle. Looking to recover lost comrades. Being a warrior is easier than waiting. Going to war is easier than talking.

Will said without opening his eyes, Only a couple of hours, less usually.

We bounced like seeds in a rattle.

I rolled a cigarette with one hand to amuse Will, lit it and handed it forward to Mau, who nodded without taking his eyes off the road, the scar on his cheek folding in two as he smoked. What did it mean to him to drive foreigners on errands he himself would never do? A dead dog rotted in a ditch. Ignorance, craving, wrong views. I have all of these. I cannot free myself from desire. I want to know. Will stared at me and I thought, I am not pretty anymore. I have gone yellow from childdeath and grief and I have become a boneless shadow. I said to Will, What do you see? He said, That this moment is good enough.

We hit a big rock and bounced and we both laughed. The dope made the wind slow down.

I had opened my whole body to you. I heard no groan of work above me, only pleasure and relief. You said once that my love released you from wishing you were dead and I believed you.

Mau stopped for a group of villagers crossing the road, pushing a house on stilts. They rolled it on four-wheeled platforms. Men pulled and pushed, ropes over bare shoulders, children ran barefoot alongside carrying sticks. In the sway of a stilt house people learn to move lightly. A woman rolling over in her sleep can sway a stilt house. A boy climbing up the steps with a heavy load can sway a stilt house. Even the wind sways a stilt house. Now the house swayed across the road, pushed and pulled by the villagers, like a traveling carnival with clowns and trained animals and acrobats and brightly robed women and barefoot men.

Will?

Yeah?

Do you think he is alive?

Do you want the truth?

Not right now.

I leaned back and felt the heat in my hair.

Another thirty kilometers down the road, a pair of three-meter-tall Kathen puppets with papier-mâché heads and pursed lip smiles and round eyes blocked the way. Enormous papier-mâché hands sliced through the air on long sticks under orange and green shirts, collecting alms for the monks. Long dresses covered the puppet bodies down to their ankles, and wide feet in sandals poked out below. The puppets swayed and reached out their hands in the middle of the road. A scatter of people ran alongside the puppets like chickens, laughing and touching the puppet dresses. Mau wanted to drive around them but they blocked the road and forced us to stop.

The male puppet stepped forward and received the money I handed to him. Everyone laughed. The female puppet walked beside the remorque reaching her hand in for more. Will jumped up and shouted in a terrible accent, Bawng! Bawng srei! and the crowd grew excited. He took the puppet hand and vaulted out onto the road, reached up and took the other hand and started to dance. Children laughed and Will called out in English to me, Look! I'm dancing for merit in the next life.

Then he dropped the puppet hand and fell back clutching his face and yelled, Aowww. My tooth! My tooth!

He twisted his head from one side to another and moaned. He fell on his knees in front of the male puppet and begged in English, Help me! Help me! I've got a horrible toothache.

The toes under the puppet spread in his sandals. The puppet knew a clown when he saw one and he reached out his hand for more alms and everyone laughed. The female puppet knelt down, swaying at the waist, reaching out both hands to hold Will's head. The crowd sighed. And the male puppet chanted a nonsense riddle:

When no judge stretches out his hand to take a coin
When every case in law is righted
When no child is found alone in an alley
When no monk takes alms from a politician
When a woman lives outside the home
And no spirit roams unburied
Then shall the world
Come to great confusion.
Then comes the time we see not yet
Of future prophecy, we live before this time.

A child ran up to the remorque and put a sweet smelling white-yellow romdoul flower in my hand. Mau called Will, Come. We must arrive before dark. As we drove away, I watched the people grow smaller in the red dust. I will never see them again, I thought. I will forget these people and they will forget me, just more barang passing through their festival. When I was young I thought I would remember everything, and now I know that people lose things in the sand and that how we tell the past and how we use the past are unconnected.

You loved the Kathen puppets. You might have explained their strange song. You knew me when my laughter hid nothing. Things do not suddenly happen to us. Things happen step by step.

I studied the red earth. I counted trees to keep awake, umbrella trees and mango trees and peacock trees. Then the road disappeared.

Memory is a bit of light on a winter wall. Yesterday while I was writing I met a distant cousin I had not seen since childhood. She had my father's mouth. Our daughter had your mouth. The travel that single day was so slow, bumping along kilometer by kilometer. And then we came to the gulley where the road disappeared and I got out of the remorque and stumbled and dropped the flower I had crushed in my palm.

The bridge broke under a truck loaded with concrete. At the bottom of the gulley, a stream ran through the cab. Bags of concrete mix were scattered down the riverbank and men were tossing what was still dry away from the water.

Will stretched stiffly, looked at the broken bridge, said, I am asking myself why the hell I came on this trip.

The truck driver's head was wrapped in bloody cotton strips. People stared. He walked in circles. Someone handed him water to drink but he shook his head and said, My truck.

I said to Will, Here is safe if you don't count landmines or holes in the road the size of moon craters or bridges that collapse or people who disappear.

Men with strong arms and backs were dragging two long tree trunks to the river. They edged them to the site of the old bridge, lifted them up and let them fall to the other side. People dragged planks up from the old bridge to begin laying them across.

I said to Mau, Let's walk across.

Mau said, The bridge is not ready yet. First they nail it.

Where are the nails? Before the nails get here we could die. It is going to get dark.

I took the handlebars of Mau's Honda 90 and pushed the moto toward the riverbank.

Mau took the handles from me and said, Yes, stop, borng srei. I will take it apart. We'll do it in two, first the wagon, then the moto. Wait, sister.

Nothing is still. Everything is moving. My mind burns with an injury that neither heals nor scars. The yellow fringe is swinging around like crazy. Everyone gathers on the riverbank to see the impatient barang. When kids run to help, Mau yells at them to get off. He and Will heave on the trailer and they do not pause and they do not rush and I watch and listen to the crack and creak of the makeshift bridge under the wheels of the small wagon. Will's shirt is wet. Mau's head is turned slightly back, the pinprick of light in his eye widened and concentrated like a horse on the bit for the first time, watching his trailer, his daily rice, his children's future. Nothing must happen to his remorque. As his foot hits the opposite shore, the front left wheel hits a knot in the wood and jams and Mau heaves the wheels of the wagon to land. A board twists up and falls in slow motion down into the gulley and Will jumps over the open spot and does a little dance. I already have Mau's motorbike on the loose planks and Mau is yelling in Khmer, Wait, sister. The boards are sliding and Will shouts, Can't you ever the hell wait?

They stand on the edge watching, leaning into the air over the makeshift bridge. I move forward step by step. I am used to pushing a motorcycle with a sidecar but Mau's bike leans. I straighten the handlebars and move toward the gap near the end. I can see the road to Ang Tasom like an arthritic finger bent away from the gulley. The back wheel hits the gap and twists. It catches and tips the bike frame sideways and the hot exhaust pipe sears my leg and I am afraid of the depth below me and the rough lines of the riverbank and I remember too having the idea that I should be down there because the dead are down there and I remember shaking myself alert and thinking I will not fall into a black hole on the road to Ang Tasom before I find you. Mau and Will are leaning out like one body and Mau grabs the front wheel and hangs on and Will grasps my wrist and hauls me to the bank. Then they both turn around to watch another board fall in a vertical slice into the cement at the bottom.

I lie sprawled on the ground and laugh. Will leans over the burn on my leg.

Now we are on the far side. Where we want to be.

58

In rice fields there are no deep currents, only what can be seen. I dab at the burn on my leg. Will rolls another joint and lights it and passes it to me. He says, For the pain.

I no longer feel pain.

A man flicks the back of his water buffalo.

I have never felt as alive as I did on the road to Ang Tasom. The yellow fringe is covered with red dust. Pretty.

If I were sitting on the roof of the FCC with you, I would order a cold beer. Later I would order a baguette sandwich and an espresso. I would touch your arm and watch men wearing leather shoes from faraway cities with those beautiful young girls who wear lipstick and heels. I would listen to the absurd things people say, watching all that human traffic. Once I saw a man pass money to another man and receive a young girl in exchange. A journalist behind me said, The wife is for children but every now and then a man needs a thirteen-year-old.

Will?

What?

If he is dead, what would be left?

Will raised his eyebrows, said slowly, It depends where the body was left. Sometimes the fat changes into grave wax, but we are almost past the rainy season, everything disappears in damp.

I think I can smell you.

59

Once a woman came to the Buddha carrying her dead son in her arms. She asked him to have mercy on her, to give her back her son. The Buddha said that he could help her. First, he said, bring me a mustard seed from a family that has never experienced death. The woman searched from home to home. People wanted to help but everyone she met had experienced death—a brother, sister, parent, husband, child. After searching for a long time the woman returned to the Buddha.

He said, Where is your son?

The woman replied, I buried him.

60

The road grew rougher. We jostled forward and I watched a young mother squatting beside the road, eating her evening meal, holding her baby. I had no baby to hold. What would she do if soldiers came up to her and grabbed her baby? The Buddha said, Hatreds do not ever cease in this world by hating, but by love. Overcome anger by love, overcome evil by good. Overcome the miser by giving, overcome the liar by truth.

Does a mother have the right to forgive the man who rips her child from her arms? Does the orphan have the right to forgive his parents' murderers? They know not what they do. Who has the right to forgive such things? Can I forgive them for taking you from me? Forgiveness is a radical act. Humans like revenge stories, even those who claim the New Testament's epic of love.

Get past the golden rule. Make the enemy inhuman. Call the enemy dog, snake, kraut, gook, kike, cockroach, slut, all that ugly talk. Tear the child from his mother and kill him or make him a soldier. Rape the woman and plant superior seed in her less than human cunt.

Mau stopped at a roadside stand to fill up his moto from one of the Fanta bottles and to buy another from narrow shelves neatly stacked with Mild Sevens and Camels and Marlboros. Will paced, restless. He picked up a stick and batted a ball of old paper around like a golf ball. In seconds a group of kids was copying him, playing golf with sticks. A girl with a limp had a nice swing.

Will called over to Mau and me resting with a cool drink by the side of the road, Meet the Takeo province junior golf team. Isn't this little girl a hummer? If I had a camera I'd take pictures and send them to Hun Sen. Do you know his favorite putter is a Kevin Burns?

Mau watched the children and spoke into the air ahead without turning to look at me. He said, You asked what happened to me. When I was a boy I spent a lot of time at the temple. I learned to read. I liked being a monk. But my family was poor and they needed me. When the killing began near us I was still fishing with my father. I was sent away from Kep because I was strong. I was sent to work carrying rocks for dams. Thousands of us carried baskets of rocks.

He pointed to the scar on his cheek. He said, I got this one day when I dropped my basket. That night I decided better to die escaping than starve here. I snuck into the women's camp and I managed to get Ary and we ran away and hid and crossed the Thai border. We spent a long time in the Sa Kaeo camp. Until the end. My wife was pregnant. Everywhere in the holding centers women were pregnant. But the Thais did not want us to have babies. The Thai camp workers started to give women a drug, Depo-Provera, and the American workers said, Do not take it, it is illegal in America.

When the Thai military came to give Ary the injection there were problems in the camp. Khmer Rouge soldiers were trying to steal food for the army. That day they forced a man to climb barefoot into an empty water tank. They closed the lid and locked it, lit a fire around it and pounded on the top with a hammer. The man screamed from inside and everyone pretended not to hear until finally one French man came and argued with the soldiers and threatened them until they opened the tank. The man was burned, half dead. I was looking for Ary and in the middle of the shouting and screaming I saw a soldier go to give her the injection. He slapped her but she did not beg. She said, Get away from me. I am sterile. I was raped so many times I am sterile.

The soldier felt such shame that he turned and walked away. This is how she tried to save our baby. By the time anyone knew, it was too late.

Mau paused, took a small sip of his drink and watched Will playing with the children. He said, I did not want my child to grow up in a refugee camp. The Thais did not want us and I had no chance to go abroad. The Khmer Rouge threatened us. They sang:

Those who go back first will sleep on cots.
Those who go back second will sleep on mats.
Those who go back third will sleep in the mud.
And those who go back last will sleep under the ground.

After the baby was born we decided we would not to stay in the camps and we walked back to Phnom Penh and I do not know why we survived. We walked close to the dead bodies and slept close to dead bodies because there the mines were already exploded. On the far side of the minefields, children sat with their skin stretched over twig ribs, waiting for parents who did not survive. We were so hungry. Our baby died on the way to Phnom Penh.

We sat side by side in the shade looking at nothing. The perfume of the romdoul flower on my palm. As if there was no trip ahead. As if we had already arrived. The end of a thing is better than the beginning. I did not know what to say. A pulse, not mine, beat through me.

Mau said, Those children, what do they know of Angka? The rice fields remind me of Angka. I drive on this long red road and I hear their songs and shouting and the sounds are burned into me. I must always be careful. I must not betray myself. You too must be careful, sister. The leaders do not want trouble.

I scratched at the earth with a little stick.

Mau stood and said, Someday even the stones will speak.

Will called, Time to go?

Mau said quietly to me, I still think of those twig children. Borng srei, I just want you to know.

61

When we were young in Montreal, after we had used up our last money at the train station taking pictures of ourselves in the photo booth, we walked across the street and went into Marie-Reine-du-Monde because the wind was so bitter off the river. We wandered under the high roof through the smoke of incense and candles. We held hands and a priest approached us and asked us not to touch in this sacred place. We looked at the murals of Catholic priests and nuns being burned alive and the shine of fire on the skin of the Indians and we studied the faces of attacked and attackers twisted in rage and agony, eyes turned up, limbs straining. We stood in the nave under a tall sculpture of a man hanging, tortured on a cross. I longed for an image of compassion in this place of worship. I stood beside you, forbidden to touch you, and sudden tears filled my eyes and you said, Do not be ashamed. When I take you to Angkor Wat you will see carvings on the walls of people suffering and falling into hell, Yama sending people to their fate. These things are everywhere.

I close my eyes even now and I can feel the heat of your palm on mine and I can smell the incense and you.

62

Mau turned and slowed down, Last wat before Ang Tasom.

I dropped some riel from the side of the remorque at the temple gate but the paper notes missed the table and fluttered in the breeze. Children playing on the roadside scooped them up, placed them on the table, turned to wave. Big smiles. Festival time. Your smile.

Drumming from Ang Tasom and the bright blur of festival crowds in the streets. Mid afternoon of the last days of Kathen and drummers dressed in yellow shirts and red ties with red sashes around their heads beat long drums decorated with red, green and gold ruffles. Old women wearing red sampot skirts and men wearing clean sarongs followed, swaying to the rhythms, under enormous lace-trimmed yellow umbrellas, carried baskets of food offerings on their heads. At the front of the Kathen procession three people wearing yellow shirts and red scarves and sashes carried stacks of folded clean saffron robes. Following behind were women and men wearing tall orange and gold and red headpieces shaped like temples. Barefoot children ran along the sides and clapped and kicked pebbles and hoped for something sweet to eat.

As the procession moved farther down the road toward the

temple we edged through the market on the main street, a row of food stalls and tables sheltered by tin roofing, covered with white and red checkered plastic, steam rising from pots of boiling water, ditches of dirty water on the roadsides. Two young mothers with their babies peeked around the pole of a stall. I watched with a dull ache the casual way they shifted their babies on their hips. Mau slowed and stopped at Thmor Sor guesthouse with its open air restaurant in front and simple outdoor toilets round back. We climbed down from the remorque and stretched and Mau said quietly, I will go now and see what I can find out and I will stay with my wife's cousin and come in the morning to find you. Wait for me here.

Will and I went into the restaurant and Will ordered more food than we needed and cold beer and bottled water and soon a little huddle of children pressed close to our table. Waiters brought plates of noodles and morning glory greens and pork and a fish I did not know. Will wrapped up a large packet of meat and fish in a napkin on his knee. He slipped it into the hand of the biggest girl of the group, who made it disappear under her shirt. The waiters watched and pretended not to see. Everyone was trying to survive. Please God, Buddha, milky stork over churning waters, please.

After we ate, I said to Will, I am going to buy something for my burn. Will nodded, said, I'll wait here. I'm going to sleep.

I walked along the road and stopped at a stall where an old woman leaned over the steam of her noodle pot and I said, I am looking for a man who was brought here during the coup six months ago. Where is the jail? Where do the soldiers from Phnom Penh bring their prisoners? I can pay.

The old woman turned away frightened. No one used the word *coup*. People called grenades *events*. She said, I do not know anything.

All through the market I asked the same questions and eyes darted and glanced away looking for who might hear, who might see. No one said anything. Everyone turned from me. I bought a salve of aloe, went back to my airless room and waited.

Just before dusk, two police officers came to the hotel. One was a young man with a clear complexion and wary eyes. The other was a short middle-aged man with hard eyes and a thick scar on his right hand. He said roughly, The chief of police wishes to speak with you.

Will came into the hall, said, What's going on? He put himself between me and the men and said in a whisper, What the hell did you do?

I stepped away from Will, said in English, So they don't have to blame Mau, so they can blame me.

In Khmer I said to the hard-eyed man, If I do not come back my friend will come looking for me. If I do not come back everyone in my country will know.

He spat to one side and the young soldier looked away embarrassed. They walked, one on each side of me, down the main street where the stalls were still open for the celebrations and people were relaxing on cool rooftops. The two men led me down a side path to the police station and escorted me into a cement block room where a man wearing a clean and pressed light blue shirt sat on a wooden chair. A single lightbulb burned overhead in the center of the room. He was heavyset with deep creases between his eyes. He did not stand up but motioned me to sit on the chair on the other side of his desk. He dismissed the two soldiers and said, What is your name?

Anne Greves.

He lit a cigarette, did not offer me one, looked across the desk at me, said, What are you doing here?

I am looking for someone who went missing.

This is not permitted.

His Khmer was formal, educated.

I understand. But I am doing it anyway. I would like to know your name.

I no longer pretended deference. I no longer pretended anything.

His gaze deepened, the only movement in his still face. He leaned forward, rested his forearms on the desk, said, My name is Ma Rith. I am the district chief of police. What makes you think you can do this?

I said, It is normal to look for someone who is missing. I know he was brought here.

How do you know?

A soldier told me.

What is his name?

He did not tell me.

Ma Rith opened an old file on his desk and wrote. He looked up again, said, Where?

He approached me in a doorway, but I do not remember exactly where. Somewhere off Sisowath Quay in Phnom Penh.

He wrote and looked up again, said in a reasonable, persuading voice, You must understand that you cannot come to Ang Tasom and ask people to talk about things of which they know nothing. It makes unrest. Our country has suffered a lot.

Our leaders must have the loyalty of the people. There can never be order without this. We are rebuilding our country and creating democracy.

The government used these ritual phrases in all their speeches. On radio broadcasts. In the papers. But they also said, If there is opposition, there will be a return to Pol Pot.

I said, In the new democracy of Kampuchea, you will want the truth to be told and justice to be done. You will understand that people cannot just disappear.

Ma Rith continued as if I had not spoken, You have been in this country for only a short time. You must go back to Phnom Penh. You cannot create trouble here.

I said, I do not want to make trouble. I only want to find out what happened.

He raised his eyebrows and his tone hardened, You must understand that the hope of finding lost family members never comes for most of our citizens. The sad perseverance of searching and not finding is something our citizens continue to suffer.

He leaned back and shifted to a softer tone, I always feel pain when I see people seeking family members separated during the wartime. I pray to the sacred objects to allow those people to meet their family members again. Some of my family members and friends have forever left me, and I still do not know exactly their fates. We have to move on.

Ritual phrases.

I saw in his eyes no pain at all, but the impatience of a man who has a job to do. When a river changes direction anything can happen. The well-ordered turns on itself. Bodies float face down in gentle eddies.

I looked into his eyes and said, I am not looking for someone lost during the Pol Pot time. I am looking for someone who disappeared from a political rally six months ago.

He dropped his cigarette on the floor, stepped on it, answered, Let us say there was an accident and the one you are looking for is dead. Since there would be nothing you could do, it would be better to go back to Phnom Penh. Our leaders and your Western leaders do not want trouble.

My bowels loosened and a crown of beads formed over my temples. I wanted to scream but there was no breath. I wanted to say, There is already trouble. People shot in the streets. Bodies left on the riverbanks. Leaders fleeing across borders.

I said, I want his remains.

I forced out the words, not believing them yet. I said, If someone dies, surely people collect their bodies. In Phnom Penh people went to the temples to claim their dead. I saw it.

He tapped his pen on the file, said, Of course there are procedures. But a person must be able to identify their dead. And if it happened that someone wished to claim disputed remains, this person would have to make a tribunal with the Ja Vei Srok in Ang Tasom.

He was trying to show there were laws, new ways that depended on neither tradition nor violence. But his words were like seeds without soil. He had to satisfy his leaders. He had to make problems disappear. He sensed my disdain, said with reined anger, In your case a tribunal will not be permitted because there is nothing to find. Now you will go back to your room and in the morning return to Phnom Penh. Your driver has been told.

He tapped his pen, bullying and harsh. The interview was over.

But I said, I wish to request your help to locate his remains.

We both watched him lay his pen deliberately on the desk. He stood and lifted his right arm above his head and brought it down with a pointing finger toward my face, slicing the air three times as he spoke.

You do not listen. There is nothing to find. You will return to Phnom Penh.

Jab. Jab. Jab.

The naked lightbulb over our heads flickered, dimmed and came back on. He did not glance at the faulty light and I closed my eyes and saw a fleeting image of a young woman looking into the eyes of her baby. I warned myself to concentrate, to get myself released. He lit another cigarette, blew smoke into my face.

He said, You will be taken back to your room. At dawn you go back to Phnom Penh. We do not want trouble.

63

I do not understand the unfathomable love I feel for you. But I am in a place the old Gnostics call emptiness. If your face appeared around the doorway where I sit at this small desk, I would turn to you and say, Now I am awake.

The strangeness of my love for you is that it has made me dead in life and you alive in death. I am afraid you will disappear and no one will remember your name.

64

After dark I heard a light scratch on my unlocked door. Mau slipped in, closed the door behind him. There was a bruise on the scar over his cheekbone. He said, I am sorry, borng srei.

It was a warning bruise, a red lettered note.

He stood inside the door and whispered, They throw bodies in the canal beside the bamboo seller's house. At the end of the road going out of town. After the grenade rally they brought two bodies. They shot him because he took pictures of the grenade throwers. They knew he had connections in the West. They did not want his body found. That is why they brought him here.

Mau's liquid eyes held mine and he lifted his hands as if to touch me then let them drop again. He said in a whisper, At least you know. Many people never find out. As soon as there is light, I must take you back. Everything is ready. You must come with me at dawn. Do not make trouble. You do not know what these men will do. I will sleep at my wife's cousin's. I must go now, they are watching me.

I slipped from the back door of the hotel and into the Kathen procession on the main street. The people's faces were illuminated by flickering candles. Drums and gongs and chhing finger cymbals grew louder, celebrating the divine. I was not part of the crowd because people shifted away from me though I walked in the middle of them. When the people turned down the path toward the temple I stepped into the shadows of the unlit road, continued to the end of town and saw the bridge over the canal. I saw cut bamboo leaning against the bamboo seller's house. Next door to the bamboo seller was a Buddhist monument maker and I saw his yard of stone carvings like a garden of spirits squatting and sitting and standing under the clouded full moon night. I slipped along the side of the little house past the old retaining wall and found an animal path down a small hill to the edge of the canal. Then I waded into the canal, afraid of what might be there.

Waist deep in the unlit night, in a world of smell. At first I did not feel the wet chill. A storm in the mind removes all feeling from the senses. I heard Mau whisper from the bridge, Stop, sister. Come back.

Someone was slipping down the bank after me and then I heard Will's voice, Get the hell out of there.

Mau pointed from the bridge down into the center of the canal. They dropped the body from a truck here, he said. Come, sister. Nothing left. Come. I am afraid of sramay.

There are no ghosts. Only you.

I waded deeper until I stood under Mau and then I looked into the blackness, Here?

He leaned over, Come out. There will be nothing. Everything washes away. Come, there are neak ta.

Spirits. And village leaders.

Mau slipped off the bridge and slid down the bank too. He

squatted on the edge, said, The leaders do not want you here. Look, someone gave me something so you would know, so you can leave.

I reached to his outstretched hand and Mau grasped my wrist and pulled me into the grasses. He pressed my old St. Christopher medal into my open palm and released my arm.

He said, The bamboo seller took it from his body. You have this proof. This is enough.

It is not enough. See what breeds around the heart.

Wings and webbed feet on the surface of the water. Forest ducks have laid their eggs in skulls in all the canals of Cambodia. Starving dogs scrounge. Rats nest.

A flock of cranes rippled through the sky.

I felt the cold of the tiny medal on my wet skin. As I turned from Mau, I tripped and the water splashed in the grasses and disturbed the hidden waterfowl whose wings beat hard against the canal. Air heavy enough to scoop with a cup. Blood pulsing behind my eyes. The burn on my leg under the water stinging. What lies beneath? I am in your grave and I am haunting you.

I turned to where Mau had crouched but there was only darkness. Will waded toward the center of the canal and he studied the water and the riverbank, said, If they dropped him from there.

Then he looked into the muck, said, Can't you ever the hell not stir things up? He glanced up at the bridge again, calculating, whispered, If they dropped him from there, he would have fallen around here. But animals move things. And there is weather.

Behind us the canal widened and Will said, Anne, there's probably nothing left but I will have a look. Keep quiet.

The place swayed with dark blowing. He walked in small circles. He knew his work. Bodies are eaten by pigs, bones scatter, sink into the silt. The trees have eyes. I listened to Will's slow concentrated breath and watched him search deliberately in the chill dark. Over and over, he squatted, neck deep in the water, dipping one shoulder down below the surface, turning his face to the side to breathe, arm tugging, back covered with water hyacinths and slime. Be quick. He pulled things up, now a stick, now a rock, once a small bone. He examined them on the surface, tossed them to shore, said, Not human. He took up his circles again. He disappeared below the surface as he worked at releasing what he found by touch in the stinking water. I waited. In the distance I heard men beating chhai-yam drums. Three things cannot be hidden, the sun, the moon and the truth. At the temple there would be theater with puppets and the lighting of candles and incense. A light breeze in the canal grasses.

After a long, long time, slowly Will lifted something. I saw him bend over it, tenderly smoothing off silt, and then he raised it above the water and I watched drops falling in silvery streams as it broke the surface. The clouds blew away, uncurtained the full moon. The end of the monsoons. Tomorrow the monks would have new robes. Pinpeat music far away.

In that wet dark place we were two creatures divided at the waist by water and I took the skull he offered me and I felt his shoulder against mine as we examined it together in the blackness. I was afraid of what I touched. I did not know the dead. How could this small piece of bone harm the world? Surely it was not you. This tiny skull could not be you, somewhere you were still alive. Then I saw a half-moon chip on a front tooth loose in the upper jaw.

65

Here hung those lips that sang. We will no more meet, no more see each other. I pulled you to me, hugged you against my breasts.

On the filthy bank of the canal in the dark-eyed night I sat in the mud to cradle your skull forever. Will squatted beside me and his finger traced the curve of the skull and pointed to a small ragged opening. He said, That is the entry hole of a bullet. Where a bullet entered the right temple.

Expertly he turned the skull while still I held it, said, There is no exit wound. If it did not lodge inside, it could have gone through the orbit of an eye. If it was lodged inside, it would fall and sink.

I held the bone and felt its curve under my palms and I looked at the pocked surface. All the joys of life left no mark at all. What is the value of a single human life? I will cremate you. I will say prayers over you.

The sand falls, not much left now, just a few last grains, and as I have watched them falling year after year after year, I do not ever come to the end. I lost you again, a third time, the last time. My sorrow and my failure.

His eyes were two dark moons. Will stared past my shoulder and under the slime and water hyacinth muck on his chest he turned into sweating stone. He whispered hoarsely to a silent shadow behind me, Bawng, muy soam. Without taking his eyes off the gun Will said to me, Get up very slowly and turn around and tell him we're leaving, we're going to the hotel and getting out of town, tell him. Tell him we're getting the hell out. Tell him.

The line between life and death disappeared. I bent over as if to hide something and Will grabbed my arm and dragged me up from the bank shouting at me, Pretend you're afraid of me, then he threw me down on the bank and turned to the men with guns, his palms pressed together, fingers up, in front of his chest, begging.

Bawng, we're going, just put your guns down.

They answered in English, You leave Ang Tasom.

One man's foot was at my head and his hand thrust down and swiped your skull from between my breasts and tossed it far down the canal, back into the water. I looked at my empty hands without believing.

I hear the light splash, like a duck landing in spring, over and over and over and over. For thirty years I have heard that splash.

66

I fell on the soldier's arm and Will pulled me off and started dragging me up the bank. The soldier said to me in Khmer, The village leaders say you must leave.

He shoved Will so hard he fell at my feet. The soldier looked me eye to eye and said in Khmer, He will take you back. Go now. No trouble. Or I come back.

I smiled, a lunatic foreigner smiling a lunatic smile, and I said, Tell the village leaders if I die in my bed tonight I will haunt them.

The soldier kicked at Will. But I was no longer wedded to life. Neither was I yet married to death. I was memory and hope calculated to their smallest ratio.

I do not remember walking back to the hotel. I remember only in my room Will sitting by the wall near the door, his long legs drawn up, drinking an Angkor beer and asking, What did you say when they let us go?

I told him ghosts would get him.

Will laughed, a strained and frightened twist of air. He said, I wonder where the hell Mau went? He looked at me and said, You know, humans are made for happiness too. A happy person too can serve the sacred. You didn't have to do this.

I remember the wet print of Will's pants on the floor after he got up and said, We're leaving. Lock the door. I am going to find Mau. I hope they haven't beat the shit out of him.

What about his skull?

It is the only time I ever saw Will angry. He said, It is time to stop, Anne. It is finished. We're getting the christ out. There won't be any more chances. We're not waiting for morning.

The echoes of drums and cymbals fell silent in the deep darkness before dawn. I left the room and went back to the canal. To bury the dead is right. I did not care what they did to me. I had no thought but one: If I could not bury you, grief would break me. I smelled the red village dust. But before I could slip down the bank and into the water, three young men closed in around me. My arms were wrenched behind my back and I smelled garlic and cheap soap and I heard a hissing voice say, Stop kicking. I kicked. I felt the first blow on my head and no one in Ang Tasom saw anything, heard anything.

They locked me in a cement block room and I sank to the floor. I was nothing. I was so thirsty. And I was so tired. I fell into a deep sleep and was instantly woken by the call of a honey buzzard outside, *pee lu pee lu*, and there were no windows but I felt in the warming air the first gray of dawn. All the living were locked in cement rooms and all the lost were drowned in canals.

Now I belonged to the wild world of the dead.

How did I offend? I only wanted to knit you back into the earth. How could it be right for pigs and dogs to tear at the skin of your face but not right for me to bury you? They said to me, Woman, you are worthless. You understand nothing. You are nothing. Your desire is nothing.

Fool. Madwoman. Victim.

67

There was a time when I could still touch your skin. Impossible to leave. Impossible to stay.

People say, It is *their* country, let them tell it.

You are my country.

Two guards came and went from the cement block room. They were young, thin, obedient, with stupid, aggressive eyes. They'd been trained to look for screws and rivets a prisoner might use to choke himself, for pens that open veins. They took my Buddha necklace. A pail stank in the corner. Filthy bowls of coarse rice hid pebbles that cracked the teeth. Carefully I sucked the rice and spit out the bits of stone. There was a shallow basin of water I feared to drink and drank anyway. I would have fought for those drops of water. When I cried of thirst an older guard said, Be quiet or I'll come back and beat you. When I turned my back on him he said, Turn so I see you or I'll beat you. He asked, Are you hungry? I said, No. Then he said, You're lying. Tell the truth or I'll beat you.

His body was possessed of an exact memory of how he kept men from killing themselves before they were tortured to death.

Someone once asked Martha Graham how she remembered her dances. She answered, The body remembers.

After I made love for the first time I understood this.

The guards searched me and I was condemned to remember.

I was a woman reduced to a T-shirt and bra, underwear and cotton pants and pain and thirst. I shivered at night and curled up in a ball wrapping my arms over my face against the rats. My leg swelled red and my head throbbed. The first night I thought, Will knows I am here. Mau knows I am here. They will come soon. On the third night I thought, Maybe no one knows I am here. They kept me awake all night, sitting up in a corner. When I dozed they woke me with water or a kick. At dawn the guard tied my hands behind my back and took me again to the office of Ma Rith.

He dismissed my guard with a sharp, Baat, tien! and gestured to the chair opposite him. His desk was empty except for his package of Marlboros, a cheap yellow Angkor lighter, his folded sunglasses and a mug of water. I wanted my tormentor's water.

He said, Why did you go back to the canal? I told you there is nothing to find.

Aching. Thirsty. Sleepless. My hands tied. Now I was a body made vulnerable. Now I was available to wound.

I said, I found him.

Ma Rith answered, You found nothing.

I shifted in the chair. I was free to say anything; I did not care if I died.

The government does not admit that any wrongdoing happens. How can people move on without knowing what happens to their families? How can they move on without truth?

The damp hot air was still between us.

Ma Rith's eyebrows lifted and then his face smoothed again. He said, Our leaders say we should dig a hole and bury the past and look ahead to the new century with a clean slate. All of us have family members, friends and relatives killed and left uncremated by the genocidal regime.

Outside, far away, the call of a vulture.

I said, What we think, we become. If the truth is not told, the spirits of the dead will never rest.

Ma Rith's voice sharpened like a string tightened across worn frets, You are not from here. Why do you come and interfere? We must accept the reality of our history. Our dead are silent and lost. Our country has suffered decades of war. We must turn from this terrible history now and build a future.

I said, People want the truth. But they are afraid. Your citizens too wish to speak for those made silent. Someone must act in the name of the lost. Why are you willing to bury the past, but not to bury those who lived in it? What law is transgressed by burying the dead? What law of nature? Of the gods? I found his skull. I recognized his tooth.

You did not find him. Whatever you found, it was not him. There are many skulls in this country. It is easy to confuse them.

He lit a cigarette and took a deep draw. He leaned back on his chair, more relaxed than the last time, provoked and bullying. I was dirty, thirsty. Outside I heard the squawks of starlings and the chirrups of tree sparrows.

I said, I only want to perform rites for him, cremate him, ask the monks to say prayers for him. It is normal to bury the dead.

A strange stillness held me, and I watched Ma Rith's shoulders tighten. I feared I had fallen asleep when I noticed him take a last draw on the stub of his cigarette and crush it with cold calm. I did not want to show weakness. I had become an animal who might die. I had become capable of anything, of sleeping while I spoke, of stealing water, of unspeakable atrocity, of acting without feeling. I had to control myself, to find a way. Please, loak borng, I said, allow me to bury his skull.

Ma Rith said, This task does not belong to you. You are a foreigner. The body belongs to his relatives in Cambodia. Why do you defy our law?

I said, He has no relatives. I claim the right to give my husband a proper burial. The law is only a man's thought. Surely you would not allow anyone to take away a family member's body and say nothing.

The air changed. I had crossed a line, passed through a door into a different room.

He smiled derisively. He shifted a pair of sunglasses on the desk and said with mocking, There is a younger brother. We know him. And we know also that he was not your husband.

I tried to push down the clench of nausea and heat and chill sweat. I glanced around the room, saw no bucket. I said in a voice no longer strong, He is my husband. Together we conceived a child.

What child? You have no child.

He did not wish to talk about babies and marriage and grew cruel, as if it were a family argument, intimacy waiting to explode into rupture, violence, silence. I paused to still my shaking voice, said, I had breakbone fever and I crossed the river too soon and my baby died. It was a girl.

He said mockingly, Do you think we do not know who you are? We know everything. We know when you came. We know what he was doing. You are not married. You are like any beer girl.

The words cut like an oxcart axle across the head.

My shoulders ached and I could not wipe my wet forehead.

I have committed no crime. My husband disappeared from a political rally in Phnom Penh. I found his skull. I want to cremate it and pray.

How far his eyes might pierce I could not tell. He had been ordered to make me comply. Suddenly he slammed his open hand on the desk and I jumped and he said in a raised voice, At oy té. You have committed a crime. You are not permitted to claim anything.

Humanity dictates burial of the dead, I answered.

Ma Rith said, Humanity does not dictate respect for the disloyal. This man was betraying his government. He deserves no loyalty.

A chill wind entered my body, through my groin, one that has never fully gone away.

I said, What is loyalty after death?

When I die, said Ma Rith without temper, I will still know my enemies.

False of heart, light of ear, bloody of hand. Is man no more than this?

I straightened on the hard chair, said, When I die, I will still know my loved ones. I will die before I leave Ang Tasom without him. I know he is here.

Ma Rith stood then, walked behind me, leaned over me. He said, No woman will tell me how to enforce the law of my own country.

My insides were liquid. The room was thick with ragged spirits. How much cruelty does it take to put out our human light? How far would this go? On the gateway over the entrance of the cemetery at Errancis is the single word, DORMIR.

I spoke to his empty chair, There is a law older than the laws of man. Divine law says: Every stranger is holy. What divine law have I broken?

He sat down again, wrote on paper thin as the eyelids of a corpse. He said, You are a victim. It is as if an accident happened to you. You say there is no one to claim him but you are wrong. His brother is alive.

The burn on my leg throbbed. But it felt like someone else's body. I was interested in the pain but it was no longer mine.

I said, Loak bou, I have only one desire: to love my dead. How can this be wrong? Your citizens would say this too, but terror makes them close their mouths. His brother does not care.

Ma Rith lit another cigarette, impatient now. This was dull theater. There were other things to do. His job was to get rid of me and still we were talking. If he could not persuade me he would force me. He closed the file and spoke once again in that soft, cajoling voice used for ritual phrases, What purpose to revisit the past?

I said, To claim the present.

He opened up his dark glasses and put them on. He said, Burn the old grass to let the new grass grow.

The earth will be burnt up, will perish and be no more.

We had pared the argument from both sides and left nothing in the middle.

You will be sent back, he said. You will be taken to the

airport and put on a plane to your country and you are forbidden to return to Cambodia.

I was taken back to the cement block room. I examined the cracks in the walls. I did not look at my own body. I observed the throb of hunger and the dizziness of thirst. I crashed into sleep. If you are there in the wild place I will walk straight to you and rest in you. Have you found your dead, your mother, your father, your grandmother, Tien, and do you sit with them? Is there music where you are? Is there rock and roll? Is my mother there? I thrashed at the rats and listened to a voice crying out in little sharp cuts from half-sleep and realized it was my own. At dawn the next day I heard a car arrive, men's feet and voices outside. Now I would be torn from you forever. I was so thirsty.

Montreal

68

My hands were bound, my body ached. On the road out of Ang Tasom, I saw Mau, waiting, half hidden behind a market stall on the roadside, and he raised his eyes to me. In the car with closed windows we crashed through rough potholes, scattered birds. My shoulders bumped against my tormentors and I tried to shrink into a body that could not be touched. I no longer smelled the sugar palm or rice paddies of Cambodia, only the stale breath of those whose duty it was to silence me.

Do you remember the girl in the yellow room on Bleury Street? Thick snow softly falling on Sunday morning sidewalks. I reached for you, expanded into your embrace. Once there were many places, but now there was only you. I loved the way you watched me in the yellow room.

I could not see our driver's eyes on the road to Phnom Penh. He wore dark glasses and his hands clenched the wheel as he bumped against rocks. Mau had driven with delicacy around the great holes and boulders of the dancing road, stopping to give alms, lifting his moto over a broken bridge, glancing over his shoulder at us, reaching back to share a cigarette.

I will never see the Elephant Mountains again but I can still see Chan's stiff hands and her twitching face. In the concrete room I learned with dread certainty: They could do with me what they wanted. They took you from me, and they diminished me to flesh, made me foreign in the world.

69

At the airport two hard-faced soldiers flanked me and a small woman with harsh hands untied my wrists and gave me a washed T-shirt and cotton pants that were too big. She watched me undress and took my filthy clothes with disgust and put them in an old bag. I was to leave with nothing. They escorted me through customs and gave me my passport and told me to write my name on a document but I would sign no expulsion order. The eyes of the official flickered not brown but slate and my bowels dissolved. These were eyes that could harm me. Four men forced me onto the plane and people stared and soldiers stood at the exits until the plane took off.

70

Leaving felt like falling into a clean bed. Grief. Exhaustion. Footsteps outside a locked door. I no longer recognized myself. I ate everything on the tray and when they offered me a second I took that too. I slept fitfully. In the plane. In my father's house. I ate at my father's table. I remember his eyes on me.

Daughter, he said, you are so thin.

I did not know the time or season, the air was cold and smelled of winter, or perhaps it was only a winter-seeming night.

I told Papa you were dead, that I found your skull. He held up his hand, said, Rest now. You can tell me everything later. When you are rested.

What he meant was, Do not tell me more.

I watched the shadows stretch over the walls of my childhood bedroom and wondered how I had come to this.

Berthe came, sat on the edge of my narrow bed, opened her arms to me and I cried. She smelled of pine-tar soap. She said, Mon p'tit chou, what have they done to you?

My father invited visitors. He was afraid of my foreignness. I sat wrapped in a frayed eiderdown on the old chair beside the lamp with the chipped shade. Charlotte came with her three children, hesitated as if she did not know me. Her children stared with wide eyes, squabbled over this color or that, broke and cried over a red crayon, filled in lines. Charlotte labored to fill my silence, and I could not tolerate her talking. When she asked, What are you going to do now? I sent them all away.

71

After I lost you, a thought formed clearly beneath the flat thunder in my head: No one can help me. Despair is an unwitnessed life. The ones who murdered you came and went, going about their business. And my trust in the world was destroyed.

No one will ever see you, still sleeping beside me, needing nothing.

72

I visited offices, clean ones, well lit ones, where men in suits came and went, opened briefcases, told me their names, consulted papers, repeated in different ways, We do not intervene against the laws of another country, there is always a chain of custody for a corpse, what makes you think a foreign national could just go anywhere and claim an unidentified skull?

The lawyer answered the telephone during our interview and spoke French and Polish as well as he spoke English. He gestured to a pile of files on his disordered desk. He said, I have clients in prisons for years without a trial. He punched a closed fist against an open palm, stood, walked to the corner of his office, looked over the river, said, You are lucky they kicked you out. You could have been stuck in prison.

I said, I committed no crime. They held me without charging me. They leave bodies unburied. People are going missing. Can you help me get back there to get his skull?

You have a dogged quality, he said.

I said, The worst humiliation is that they kicked me out. They think, Let her go, no one will care once she is out.

People like you cause trouble when you are in prison, he said. I care, but I do not know what more I can do for you.

The authority of any government stops at its citizens' skin. People everywhere look for their missing. We see the women of the plazas. We see women standing on the edges of graves. We hear the dignified plea, Can no one find me even a bone to bury?

It has become so easy to see. Images in the air we breathe. People know what is going on.

The question that skitters over me like rats in a prison cell at night is this: Once we know, what do we do?

This is what I know: You keep coming back to me.

73

For thirty years, silence has strangled me from the inside and I peck at the shell trying to break it, trying to be born without drowning. Silence. A crime. I have done exactly as they wanted, moved on as if nothing happened. But, borng samlanh, you too did exactly as they wanted; you made yourself vulnerable enough to die. For so long I have felt shame. I have watched myself living as if from outside my body, pretending to be alive. I tried to live, worked, married, gave birth to two sons. My husband left, said it was a mistake, said I was remote. I raised my sons, cooked Sunday dinners for my father. I never told what happened to me over there, not all of it. Papa loved me the best way he could. He took my sons fishing in the Gatineau. I used to stand at the door and watch them climb into his car, all three of them wearing their fishing hats. Now I know the anguish of watching a child go. All my bone wanted to leave home when I was sixteen, and when my sons wanted to leave, all my bone wanted them to stay. This is the genius of: *For he so loved the world he gave his only begotten child.* My father watched who he thought I was disappear in front of his eyes. He could never bring himself to ask who I became. And I did not tell him.

74

I refused, for years, to see Will when he traveled through Montreal, but I met him by chance one day on St. Laurent. I recognized him when I saw him shift a small backpack from one shoulder to the other. The crevices on his cheeks had deepened. The heels of his hands were red. The clean light in his eyes shone past a life of too much alcohol and nicotine and jet lag and the labor of releasing the missing from their graves.

He said, You look good. You never change. Want a drink?

Will always made me laugh. My hair is thin. The veins on the backs of my hands are knotted. Will had found a man who would unpack his plastic bags filled with death-stinking work clothes, who would live with the severed limbs in his nightmares. We spoke of work and failed marriages, my children, his lover. He drank his first beer quickly and poured another, said, Why wouldn't you see me?

I looked down the street. Are you happy?

Will laughed, Happiness is not that important.

I remembered how much I had once liked him.

We sat in silence, remembering, and he said, You still love him, don't you?

I looked into his eyes and had to look away. After a moment

I said, Last week my father died while he walked to work. An aneurysm in the brain.

Will put his stained hand over mine.

At the hospital, I asked for a pan of warm water and soap and clean towels and I washed my father's body. There was a bruise on his cheek from his fall. I had never seen his genitals. The thin graying hair. I had never touched his feet. He was a modest man. I had not stroked his face since I was a small child. I had loved his eyes, his hands, the brown spots of aging. I washed the muscles of his forearms. He died going to the hospital to work on a leg to help a small boy run. While I washed him I wanted to say to someone, Look. Look, his hands were skilled. I covered him with a clean sheet and I went to his apartment, found his best clothes, went to the funeral home to dress him. His body was so cold. It takes strength to move the heavy limbs of the dead. The mortician said, You do not have to do this.

I sat with his body all through the night. The funeral director said, You do not have to stay.

I accompanied his body to the crematorium and I saw the heavy doors open and I watched him disappear this last time without his usual shy smile. It made a crater in me, hollow, echoing, numb, arid, void. I signed papers and I received his ashes and I buried them. It took three days.

Will said, Do you know that when an infection gets bad enough even bone starts to disintegrate. The skin swells and the bone goes soft and breaks down into mush.

He picked up his glass, took another sip and said, For love's sake, tell before there is nothing left.

75

I remember you bent over the two strings of your chapei playing for a girl with long kinked hair. I have the two little pictures of you and me taken in the picture booth in the train station near the church. Cassette recordings of your voice. Nothing else.

I have lived in intimacy with the violence of the untold life.

Not long ago I sat for ten hours, watching a screen. I did not doze. Each person who was photographed and died in Tuol Sleng prison is posted, five thousand pictures, each lasts five seconds before dissolving to black. When I closed my eyes that night I had after-images of eyes and the strange twist of the shoulders and neck when the arms are tied behind the back. And I heard your voice.

My colleagues gossip together, Has she not had a marvelous life? Those early years of travel, where was it? Viet Nam? Thailand? Somewhere over there. And two sons and her gift for teaching languages and her writing cabin by the river in the Gatineau. She says she writes but she never publishes anything.

Light laughter.

Her marriage did not survive, but whose does anymore?

More light laughter.

She never seems to lack for friends.

Did you hear? Her father just died.
He must have been quite old.
N'importe! At any age it is affecting.
Still.

76

Only I can see you now. Candles on the river. I waited for you, and for a while this was enough. But you did not come back to me. When it was time, I knew the way to you, and I knew where you would be. You gave me flower buds wrapped in a leaf and we listened to music and when we walked on the river it turned around and flowed back to where it began.

77

I do not listen to the old music, the almost forgotten sound of those young Khmer musicians recording as fast as they could write, getting it all down live. None of your musician friends survived, all were left on the streets for dogs, dumped in mass graves. I once wondered when I saw the skulls at Choeung Ek if I was looking at any bone from which that hope-filled music came.

Now, borng samlanh, I see in the mirror a woman of a certain age. I have filled in time since the day I lost you. A lifetime of silent pretending.

If we live long enough, we have to tell, or turn to stone inside. I try to release you from a pit in my heart but unburied and unblessed you imprison me.

I long for the brush of your fingers on my skin. I long for the light of your eyes. If I pray, I pray to a wounded god. In the end it is only the wounded who endure. In Cambodia they say, Loss will be god's, victory will be the devil's.

78

You keep coming back to me in little bits of moving images, light on a winter wall. Come to the door, spirit I know, and I will stand and hold you. Come alive just one more time, let me feel your breath, Serey, let me hear your voice in song, let me wash away the pain. Come, and I will whisper your name to you one more time.

HISTORICAL NOTE

This novel takes place during the Cambodian genocide (1975–79), in which two million people died, through the Vietnamese occupation (1979–89) and into the United Nations Transitional Authority, which was to supervise the administration of Cambodia and to attempt to create conditions for the first democratic election in 1993. Those who oppose the government continue to be killed.

Historical timelines have been compressed for this fictional story.

ACKNOWLEDGMENTS

My reading about Cambodia's and other countries' genocides and truth commissions, and survivors' and perpetrators' reflections, is woven through the fabric of this story. The responsibility for this story, however, is mine, and all allusions to other writers' reflections and witness accounts have been transmuted here into the kind of truth that fiction tells.

I would like to acknowledge the support of a McGeachy Scholarship from the United Church of Canada.

I am especially grateful for the work of Youk Chaang at the Documentation Center of Cambodia (DC-Cam); Brad Adams and Human Rights Watch; Mark Gergis and his music collection; Rich Garella and Eric Pape's article "A Tragedy of No Importance"; Kathy Gruspier for conversation and field notes from the Ontario coroner's team; Kim Kieran for her diaries (unpublished); for photographs and the most generous consulting, Sonia Tahieri, Ton Paeng and Robert Fiala; Craig Etcheson; research from DC-Cam and the report "Documentation Center of Cambodia Forensic Project" and Yale University's Cambodian Genocide Data Bases.

Of many books about Cambodia, I wish to acknowledge especially Vann Nath's *A Cambodian Prison Portrait: One Year in the Khmer Rouge's S-21*, his art and remarkable spirit; Dith Pran's *Children of Cambodia's Killing Fields;* David Chandler's *Voices from S-21: Terror and History in Pol Pot's Secret Prison;* Craig Etcheson's *After the Killing Fields: Lessons from the Cambodian Genocide;* Human Rights Watch/Asia's *Cambodia at War* and François Ponchaud's *Cambodia: Year Zero.* I would like to acknowledge Sophearith Chuong's "Grandmother of 'Fertilizer'" (DC-Cam) as a source for Chan's fictional story on page 102, and Ralph Lemkin, who invented the word *genocide*, as the source of the quotation on page 172 ("If women, children and old people were being murdered a hundred miles from here ..."). I would like to acknowledge the work of Vann Nath with director Rithy Pan in the film *The Khmer Rouge Killing Machine* as the source for dialogue with former prison guards in Tuol Sleng on pages 131–132.

Readers who love Buddy Guy, Etta James and Sophocles' *Antigone* may hear echoes of their song and poetry. "Truth is as old as God ... / And will endure as long as He, A Co-Eternity" (page 65) is by Emily Dickinson. I have alluded to the thought of Jean Améry in *At the Mind's Limits.* I believe it was Hannah Arendt who first said, "The authority of any government stops at its citizens' skin" (page 220), and Simone Weil who wrote about *The Iliad*, "Force turns the one subjected to it into a thing" (page 32). Tzvetan Todorov wrote in *Facing the Extreme: Moral Life in the Concentration Camps,* "There is, however, no necessary correlation between how we tell of the past and how we use it; that it is our moral obligation to reconstruct the past does not mean that all the uses we make of it are equally legitimate."

Others I would like to thank are Lin Chear, Debby deGroot, Shaun Oakey, David Ross, Elizabeth Schmitz, Sally Reardon, Cheryl Carter, Paulette Blanchette, Anne Simpson, Alex Levin, Barbara Jackman, Janice Blackburn, Peter Jacobsen, Rory Cummings, The Very Reverend Bruce McLeod, the late Dr. and Mrs. N.K. Campbell, Ian Small, Michelle Oser, Linda Gaboriau and the Banff Centre for the Arts, Monica Pereschi, Josephine Rijnaarts, Manfred Allie, the Khmer Buddhist Centre of Ontario, Leslie and Alan Nickell, Adam and Ann Winterton, Madeleine Echlin, Paul Echlin, Randy and Ann Echlin, Mark and Joanne Echlin.

To Ross Upshur, true gratitude for your insights and discussion, for sharing with me the dailiness of writing. To Olivia and Sara Upshur, thank you for daily joy.

A special thank you to Sandra Campbell for invaluable criticism and inspiration over many years. You have seen this story in a thousand lights.

To David Davidar and Nicole Winstanley, thank you for your talent, editorial imagination and risk-taking. You are true well-jumpers.

And thank you to a woman whose name I never learned. In a Phnom Penh market you broke silence and asked me to remember with you.

I imagine us in a place that could forgive us all.

The Disappeared

A Penguin Readers Guide

ABOUT THE BOOK

"This thing is true: time is no healer." This biting phrase exemplifies not only the gravity of Kim Echlin's third novel, *The Disappeared*, but also the lyrical prowess of its author, who can express monumental events and emotions with just one line. (In fact, some of her chapters are just that.) Through her narrator, Anne Greves, Echlin brings to life a raw, passionate story set against the aftermath of the 1970s Cambodian genocide—the slaughter wherein some two million people perished under the murderous Khmer Rouge regime.

Anne is only sixteen when she first meets Serey, a captivating musician from Cambodia who is five years her senior and working in Montreal as a math tutor. Their attraction is erotic, and they quickly begin an all-consuming relationship. Contrary to Anne's father's wishes, the two blissfully spend days on end in Serey's apartment, making love, listening to music, and sharing stories. Written almost as a personal letter to the seldom-named Serey, the book chronicles a love affair that goes on to span a lifetime, with the narrative moving fluidly between decades, sometimes within the same page, as Anne recounts her most intimate thoughts.

Serey had been sent to Canada to escape his country's political turmoil, and as the only one in his family to get out before all communication was cut off, he has been captivated by thoughts of home. And so when, after four long years, the borders are finally reopened, Serey is compelled to return, leaving Anne in Montreal.

More than ten years pass without any word. Still passionately in love with Serey, Anne learns the Khmer language and then embarks on her first journey to find her beloved.

She arrives in Cambodia's capital, Phnom Penh, at a tumultuous time for the city: it is preparing for the country's first democratic election. Anne soon befriends a local taxi driver named Mau, and with his help she is eventually able to find Serey. They seem to resume their relationship where they left off, but much has changed—in Serey's life and in Cambodia itself. Serey lives a separate life from Anne during the day, and at times he is distant. Although he tries to shield Anne from the horrors he has come to know, she finds a way to visit the Killing Fields, called Choeung Ek, as well as the notorious Tuol Sleng prison where thousands were killed. And yet through all of this they discover a slow, gentle rhythm to daily life and once again find joy in being together.

In the book's penultimate section, Anne sets out to find Serey after he once again goes missing following an explosion at a public rally. Along the way she learns more about his secret life and encounters first hand the ongoing power struggles in Cambodia. As *The Globe and Mail* put it, "Emerging from those final pages is an act of love, and an image of horror, that elevates *The Disappeared* to a level of tragic intensity that it had been bound for from its opening sentences." In the novel's closing pages Anne returns to Montreal, where she attempts to continue the agonizing task of simply living.

Named one of eight essential spring books by *The Walrus* magazine, *The Disappeared* will keep you up at night no matter what the season. Somehow Echlin has deftly interwoven the chilling barbarism and incredible beauty of humanity into a seamless tale of one woman's lifelong journey of love and yearning for her own "disappeared." ■

AN INTERVIEW WITH KIM ECHLIN

Q: Did you spend time in Cambodia before or during the writing of this book? How long did the research take? The book's epigraph by Vann Nath, one of the only survivors of Tuol Sleng prison, is "Tell others." Why did you use that?

I travelled in Cambodia for a short time with a medical research group working on inoculation programs for children. During my visit I was moved by the various memorials to those lost during the Khmer Rouge time, almost thirty years before. From large museums, such as Tuol Sleng in Phnom Penh, to small, hand-written signs nailed to trees out in the countryside, people expressed a powerful will to "not forget." I met a woman in a market who told me the story of losing her entire family, and when I responded, "Can I help? What can I do?," she answered, "Nothing. I just want you to know." Vann Nath said "Tell others," and my experience in Cambodia was that many people wanted the truth to be told.

It seems to me that an individual's hope for freedom and justice exists almost independently of any particular political regime. Under a repressive regime, people will resist covertly if they can. In less repressive regimes, people will speak up. The current trials in Cambodia are the result of international pressure as well as the openly expressed desire for these trials by Cambodians like the artist Vann Nath, or Youk Chaang, who continues to gather information for DC-Cam (Documentation Centre of Cambodia). Of course, *The Disappeared* is a work of fiction; every country has stories of injustice and "disappeared," including Canada, where we're currently witnessing the Indian Residential Schools Truth and Reconciliation Commission. The work to protect freedom is ongoing. ■

Q: Delving into the stories behind the Khmer Rouge must have been difficult. Did you find it was at times too painful to think about or too all-consuming?

So many people I talk to about *The Disappeared* have told me personal stories of their own or their family's struggles with oppressive regimes. The question of *when* and *how* to remember comes up over and over again. There's an old Grimm's fairy tale called "The Singing Bone," in which the bone of a murdered man is dug up many years later, and, when blown on, sings its own story. In our oldest stories we see the need to believe that the truth does come out. Even when it is painful.

But to your question. After World War II, the philosopher and musicologist Theodor Adorno famously wrote, "To still write a poem after Auschwitz is barbaric." Many years later he softened this, saying that "Perennial suffering has as much right to expression as the tortured have to scream."

Writers began to respond to the events of World War II very soon after the war's end, including Paul Celan in his poem "Death Fugue," but in many cases it took years for this writing to be published and translated. In no way do I think that bearing witness to atrocity through art gives undue notice to perpetrators. But I can see that sometimes it takes years for people to be able to hear the stories.

There are some beautifully written and devastating memoirs of the Khmer Rouge years from Cambodia, as well as wonderful theatre, dance, and music. We have stories from Mao's China that the Chinese call "scar literature" and memoirs and literature from Argentina and Chile called *testimonio*. In Canada we have had several commissions that collect the stories of groups who have suffered here, particularly during periods of war.

Each group's story is particular. But a common thread that connects all of them is the belief that people affirm themselves through storytelling. Stories teach and delight. They allow both speaker and listener to become more conscious, to know history, to reflect on moral and ethical questions. Yes, reflecting on these stories is painful. ∎

Q: Language is always paramount in your novels. Did you study Khmer to better understand your characters and the setting of the book?

The challenge in this book was to find a language that could tell the stories from the genocide and accurately reflect Khmer culture. I wrote many, many drafts, and had very good linguistic and cultural consultants in Cambodia.

During the writing, I experienced a loss of language until a wonderful translator and mentor, Linda Gaboriau, said to me, "Take me into the centre of the darkness, show me what it is." After that, I reread the testimony of those who have suffered in war or genocide, and I noticed that the style of telling is very pared down. People say, "I was tortured," "I was raped," "I was thrown in a mass grave and managed to get out." There is little embellishment, no metaphor, little description beyond the plain recounting of the event. I wanted my style to reflect this kind of language: spare, essential. This is the place language begins, in very direct communication between two people.

And then I noticed that some of the greatest love poetry also has this spare, essential quality. The oldest written love poems in the world, Inanna's songs of love from Sumeria ("My love, your eyes are beautiful, your face is sweet") or those from the Bible's Song of Solomon ("O, that you would kiss me"), as well as love lyrics in contemporary music (The Beatles' "She Loves You"), use direct, unadorned language. It seems that our deepest, most intense experiences belong to a place that language can hardly reach. When this is so, I think the rhythms that hold the individual words together become very important. ∎

Q: The first half of the book reads almost as a love letter to Serey. Most people can only dream of the kind of love shared between Anne and Serey. Do you really believe in such heightened romantic love, or that there is a single person we are meant to be with?

I think we meet many people through our lives that we are "meant to be with," if we are open. In a certain way, I was meant to meet the woman in the Phnom Penh market who shared her experience with me, but that encounter could only have happened as a result of many other people in both our lives who inspired us—her to speak out, me to listen. In that brief, chance moment, one could say we were two souls meeting.

When Serey calls Anne his destiny, he is speaking in a romantic context. But his words were more prophetic than perhaps he knew in the beautiful moment of falling in love. Anne and Serey are lovers before either of them can know that their shared destiny will end with Anne being the sole person in the world who knows, and finally tells, Serey's story. Without her, he would have been murdered and forgotten. Without him, she would not have known the love that does not seek to alter. So destiny and memory transcend time and become linked. ■

Q: Many of the characters—most prominently Anne, Serey, and Sokha—lose loved ones in the war (or under warlike circumstances) and are profoundly traumatized by it. How do you think an individual can overcome an inner agony as deep-seated as theirs?

This is a big question. It may be that the answer is as individual as each person. Serey joins an opposition movement; his brother Sokha rejoins the army. Anne searches for the truth of her particular situation and is forced to confront the universal questions we find in *Antigone*: How do we live in the conflicting, and often irreconcilable, interests of the state and the individual? Does the state have the right to deny the individual human desire to name and honour their dead?

To speak about overcoming trauma, I would defer to Jean Améry, an Auschwitz survivor and the author of *At the Mind's Limits*. Améry wrote, "Whoever has succumbed to torture can no longer feel at home in the world." He writes that trust cannot be regained, that the tortured stay tortured. None of the characters in my story "overcome" their traumas of loss or pain or betrayal. For this reason, the novel is about language and memory, about how our use of language is a moral choice. Do we use the language of propaganda that renders the other less than human? Do we use the language of resistance in order to keep revealing the truth? For as Camus writes in *The Rebel*, the language of rebellion "reveals the part of man which must always be defended." Do we use memory to name the dead, to remember their stories, to work toward justice? ■

Q: Was it difficult to keep the story's focus on Anne and her perspective, and not delve too deeply into the politics of the time?

After the Pol Pot regime (1975–1979) and the withdrawal of the Vietnamese, the United Nations Transitional Authority was mandated to supervise the administration of Cambodia and to attempt to create conditions for a democratic election in 1993. The work was very complex. There was starvation and sickness; huge numbers of refugees were living on the borders. Most of the country's educated people—the artists, the Buddhist monks—were killed. Roads and bridges had been destroyed, farming was in disarray. The country was (and still is) heavily mined. There were many different political factions who used violence and force to achieve power. There was a generation or more of young people who had been separated from their families and indoctrinated by the Khmer Rouge, and large numbers of young men who knew nothing but war.

What I wanted to tell is the story of complex turbulence that accompanies a shift in political systems: how the

defence of freedom and individual rights requires
continual vigilance (and opposition when things go
wrong), how secretive governments create the conditions
for the breakdown of human rights. These are conditions
we see all over the world, the West included. When innocent citizens of democratic nations can be extradited and
tortured, as happened to Canadian Maher Arar, when the
military forces representing democratic nations can prac-
tise torture in hidden prisons as we all witnessed at Abu
Ghraib, then we can be sure of this: Individual human
rights are everyone's responsibility, and people around the
globe must find the courage to speak and to resist their
own governments if freedoms are corrupted or devolve.

But *The Disappeared* is a novel, Anne's story. I wanted
these issues to be told through her individual story and to
make the particular politics implicit in that story. ∎

Q: This book and your previous two novels, *Elephant
Winter* and *Dagmar's Daughter*, revolve around
strong female characters. Do you see any similar-
ities between them?

I like these strong female characters. When I talk with readers I feel an enormous appetite in women to explore both
their strength and their emotional connectedness, which
still tend not to be honoured in the dominant culture. I
like telling stories of women who act on their passions. ∎

Q: Can you tell us what you're working on now?

I'm currently working on new fiction and a new non-
fiction book that brings together my research on the
"literature of testimony." I think it was Elie Wiesel, the
writer and Holocaust survivor, who wrote, "If the Greeks

invented tragedy, the Romans the epistle and the Renaissance the sonnet, our generation invented a new literature, that of testimony." This is a phrase that South American writers such as Chile's Ariel Dorfman have adopted. And so, in this non-fiction book, I'm looking at examples from the literature of testimony that have moved me—in truth commissions, in plays and novels—and thinking about what it means. ■

DISCUSSION QUESTIONS

1. Anne says, "What I learned from my mother was that those we love can disappear suddenly, inexplicably. And then there is nothing." How do you think this belief affects the way Anne lives her life?

2. In Montreal, Serey says to Anne, "I like how you speak your mind and do not try to please me. Your mind is not Asian at all." Discuss the ramifications of this sentence for Anne and Serey's relationship in Montreal and in Cambodia.

3. Years into their relationship, Serey says, "Do you remember in those days, the shock of an Asian guy with a white girl, or a black with white, or a French with English, all of us pretending nothing was forbidden?" At another time, Anne says, "I never felt any forbiddenness of race or language or law. Everything was animal sensation and music." Do you think their attraction was wrapped up in the appeal and inherent danger of "the other"?

4. When Anne learns of Serey's secret life working for the opposition, she is surprised. Do you feel that they really knew each other, or were they "putting on a face" for the other?

5. Serey joins an opposition movement, his brother Sokha rejoins the army, and Anne searches for the truths inherent in her particular situation. Discuss

how these individuals try to balance the conflicting and often irreconcilable interests of the state and the individual.

6. Early on in the story Anne says, "I learned the prayers but not to pray." Discuss Anne's relationship with faith and spirituality as it unfolds throughout her life.

7. Would you say Kim Echlin believes that history shapes us or that we shape history? How is this manifested in *The Disappeared*?

8. How is parenthood characterized in this story?

9. How were you affected by reading about the genocide in Cambodia? Did you already know about Pol Pot and the Khmer Rouge, or did the story help to educate you about what happened there?

10. Did Serey challenge your notions of good and evil?

11. Anne says, "I would never be that self again. I was drowning in you. I would keep going back to you. Impossible not to." Did her love for Serey sabotage any chance she had for a new life after his death? Can someone ever fully recover from such a loss?

12. Eventually Anne is the sole person in the world who knows Serey's story. Why does she decide to tell it? Does she find comfort for herself through doing so? And what is likely to happen to Anne now that she has given us her testimony?

SUGGESTED FURTHER READING

Kim Echlin has drawn from a wide literary tradition of reflecting on history and conscience. Here are some of the works by writers whom she admires:

Fiction
Ma Jian, *Beijing Coma*
Ariel Dorfman, *Death and the Maiden*
Eduardo Galeano, *Century of the Wind*
Milan Kundera, *The Unbearable Lightness of Being*
J.M. Coetzee, *Disgrace*
W.G. Sebald, *Austerlitz*
Michael Ondaatje, *The English Patient* and *Anil's Ghost*

Non-Fiction
Václav Havel, *Open Letters*
Jorge Semprún, *Literature or Life*
Uwe Timm, *In My Brother's Shadow*
Tzvetan Todorov, *Facing the Extreme*
Jean Améry, *At the Mind's Limits*